Frogs and Snails and Big Dog's Tales

Books by Author:

Man in the Middle
Frogs and Snails and Puppy Dog's Tales
Frogs and Snails and Big Dog's Tales

Coming:

Frogs and Snails and Old Dog's Tales.

Frogs and Snails and Big Dog's Tales

A Children's Book for Adults

Short Stories from Ireland

By

Frank Murney

Order this book online at www.trafford.com
or email orders@trafford.com

Most Trafford titles are also available at major online book retailers.

Printed in the United States of America.

ISBN: 978-1-4269-6137-3 (sc)
ISBN: 978-1-4269-6354-4 (hc)
ISBN: 978-1-4269-6138-0 (e)

Library of Congress Control Number: 2011905568

Trafford rev. 07/13/2011

www.trafford.com

North America & international
toll-free: 1 888 232 4444 (USA & Canada)
phone: 250 383 6864 • fax: 812 355 4082

'Book 2 of the Newry Tales Series'

During the late 1950s and early 1960s, Red Morgan and Po Hillen are in their early teens and truly experiencing life in the Irish border town of Newry. In fact, they've become more outrageous and humourous than ever.

Uncle Luigi's Café—where their close friend and conspirator, Anto Falsoni, works part-time for his uncle—serves as the headquarters for all the gang's mischievous and devious planning, which seems to be an everyday occurrence. New and exciting interests influence the boys' lives. They race home-made carts at breakneck speeds on Newry's steep hills. Sports, mainly Soccer and Gaelic football, were a big interest and at times the boys travelled to both Dublin and England to watch their teams play. And, of course, girls and dating play a new role, and these distractions lead to some unexpected, hilarious, and sometimes embarrassing situations.

Frogs and Snails and Big Dog's Tales takes a nostalgic romp through the 1960s while sharing the daily exploits of Red, Po, and their gang—their love lives, school days, and friends, as well as other unbelievable and hilarious escapades.

Dedicated to the memory of

Patsy and Kathleen

Special thanks to

Sharon Oseas
Hazel Abdulla
and
Joyce Harvey

For their generosity of time,
encouragement
and talent.

Characters

Due to the fact that the same characters appear in almost all the stories within, I hope it may be advantageous to describe them in advance rather than in each individual story.

Anto	*Antonio Falsoni*	Well built with black hair, swarthy complexion. He had a husky voice and quite a strong personality. He lived and worked in his uncle's café, Uncle Luigi's. Good sense of humour and was the 'Bookie' of the gang.
Blackie	*Keith Havern*	Tall, well built, and athletic. Black short hair and always well dressed. A very good looking young man.
Boots	*Peter Markey*	Small, thin, with dark hair that always seemed to stick up at the crown of his head. A good footballer and loved wearing boots, hence the nickname.
Dunno	*Peter McManus*	Small, brown haired lad, best mate of Jumpy Jones. His answer to most questions was, 'Dunno'.
Ginger	*Thomas McVerry*	Small ginger haired lad with a round 'cheeky' face. A good footballer and runner. He was an excellent climber.
Jammy	*Tommy McAteer*	A dark haired, good looking lad who was an excellent footballer and a good all round athlete. He was fond of chatting up the girls. Very lucky or 'Jammy'.

Jumpy	*Francis Jones*	A tall skinny blond lad. Rivalled his mate Dunno in the brains department, but with a good sense of fun. Could never stand still and was always being asked to stop jumping around.
Lanky	*John Larkin*	A tall thin lad with large blue eyes and blond hair. Ungainly in posture but a good runner.
Naffy	*Leo McKay*	A small, mostly untidy, dark haired young man forever looking to borrow things, mostly money. A wheeler dealer.
Pajoe	*Patrick Joseph McArdle*	Red Morgan's uncle, Small, grey haired stout man with a round ruddy face. Always in a jolly mood. Carpenter by trade.
Po	*Oliver Hillen*	Small with black curly hair, hooked nose and a swarthy complexion. He was the 'ideas' man of the gang, a few months older than Red. It was never discovered where the nickname 'Po' came from but Red suspected it had something to do with his 'Potty' when he was a baby.
Red	*John Joseph Morgan*	A tall, well built, athletic lad with a mass of red hair that was unkempt during the week, but well Brylcreemed for the dances at the weekends.
Roberto	*Roberto Falsoni*	Small, balding, swarthy, stubby man who worked in the café for Uncle Luigi, mostly with Ice Cream sales. In his early 40s. Uncle Luigi's son.

Shifty	*Jimmy McShane*	Small, brown haired, freckle faced young man who enjoyed gambling. Always on the look out for ways to make money.
The Bishop	*Peter Keenan*	Tall, rather studious lad with glasses. Dark blond hair, always neat, took pride in his dress. Everyone thought he looked like a clergyman. Good Chess player.
Topcoat	*James Anderson:*	The odd one out in the gang. A small, thin, wizen faced man with a lisp and a mop of ginger hair. He was about 40 years old and lived in a little cottage on his own outside Camlough village. Would have been considered eccentric.

Places

Due to the fact that many of the same places appear in almost all the stories within, I hope it may be advantageous to describe them in advance rather than in each individual story.

Uncle Luigi's Cafe	Situated on Newry's main street, Luigi's was a local meeting place for all the gang. One of Red and Po's best friends, Anto Falsoni, worked there part-time for his uncle and café owner, Luigi Falsoni. The café had an ice cream counter on the left when entering. Next on the left was the Jukebox. On the right there were five 'Snugs' with high backed seats with a fixed table in the centre. On the left of the café was a collection of gingham covered tables and chairs. At the far end was the 'Chip Counter'. There could be found Luigi's pride and joy, the great glistening chrome chipper. It had a painted Italian beach scene on its upper part, and the same chipper was said to produce the best 'Fish and Chips' in Ireland.
The Bucket	An old, flat roofed hall found halfway along Castle Street at the corner of the hill of Hyde Market, directly facing the famous McCann's Bakery. The hall itself was said to have been originally the Abbot's house. There was a tunnel running from the building under Castle Street to the old Abbey grounds which was said to be the way the Abbot went every morning to say mass, as he was not allowed to be seen by the public. The dance floor was upstairs and was reached by a steep climb of thirty steps at the Hyde Market end. A large cross was positioned in front of the hall looking down towards the town.
The Florentine	Known as 'The Flo' , it was located at the centre of Hill Street, a well known local, Italian owned cafe, famous for its frothy coffee and good quality food.

The Savoy Cinema	Located at the corner of Monaghan Street at the canal bridge. The most modern of the local cinema's that was well known for its balcony or as it was known locally, 'The Gods'.
The Imperial Cinema	Located on The Mall. The smallest of the local cinemas and without doubt, the most ancient. When the time came to start the movie, the ticket collector would walk to the stage and open the heavy velvet curtains to expose the screen to allow the movie to begin. Known locally as 'The Flea Pit'.
The Frontier Cinema	Located on John Mitchell Place, a continuation of the main street, Hill Street. This was a favourite for a number of reasons. Firstly, it was only a few hundred yards from Castle Street. Secondly, Red and Po had found a way to gain entrance without having to pay. Thirdly, they had a morning session every Saturday in which there was a Talent Competition on stage for the local kids before the movie began. They also were well up to date on all the Serials, like The Lone Ranger, Superman, Batman and Robin, and such like.
The Nun's Graveyard	A large park type hillside behind St. Clare's Convent. It was surrounded by an eight foot wall. Inside the wall were well kept grassy areas with plants and many large oak trees and weeping willows. Looked upon as a 'spooky' place at night.
The Parochial Hall	Located at Downshire Road, near the Town Hall, this was a place which booked the top Showbands in Ireland. Every weekend it would be packed to hear music from The Royal, The Freshmen, The Miami, The College Boys, The Clipper Charlton and many more. No alcohol was served, just coffee, tea, soft drinks and milkshakes.

Newry Town Centre 1950

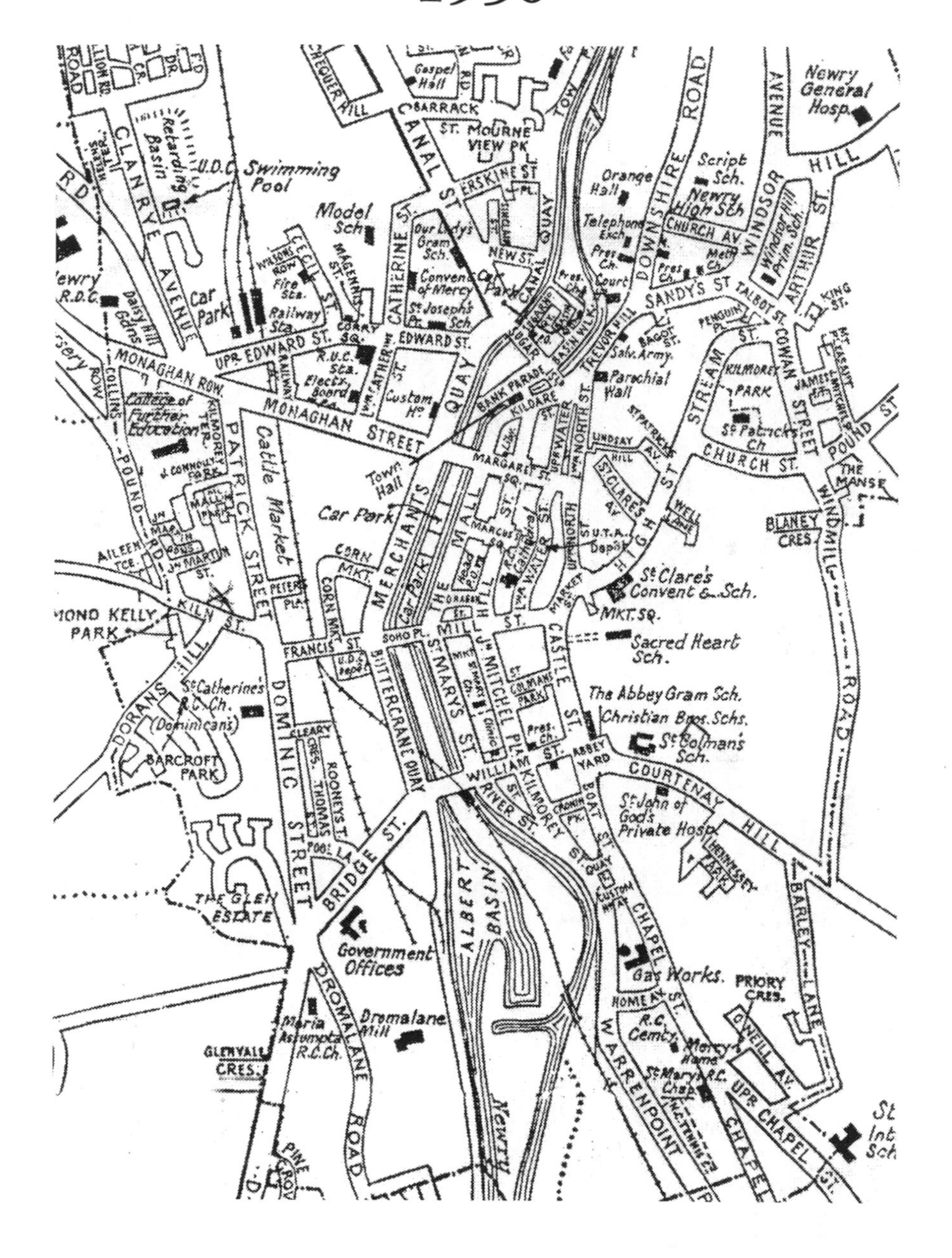

Contents

The Banshee

1960

Red was having breakfast in his house on Castle Street that Saturday morning, when the kitchen door opened and in came Mrs. McGrath who lived a few doors away. She was a large woman with a voice to match and was perhaps the only lady on the street who wore make-up every day. Red's grandmother, Ellie Morgan, was buttering some bread at the large kitchen table.

"Did ya hear it Ellie?" she asked.

"Hear it? It kept me awake all night so it did."

"Have ya heard of anyone goin'?"

"Not yet, though a heard that Mrs. O'Brien down Hyde Market was very low."

"Did ya hear it Red?" asked Mrs. McGrath.

"Hear what?"

"The Banshee."

"Never heard anythin', when was this?"

"She started wailin' about two o'clock this mornin'."

"And what does it mean then?" asked Red.

Mrs. McGrath and Ellie both made the sign of the cross at the same time.

"She has come to forewarn of death. She has come for Mrs. O'Brien, God bless her and have mercy on her soul," whispered Ellie.

Both again made the sign of the cross.

"That's what a told ma John this mornin', it has ta be poor Lillie O'Brien."

"But why would this Banshee come ta tell ya Mrs. O'Brien's dyin', it could be anybody, couldn't it?" asked Red.

Red's grandmother sat down and crossed herself again.

"The Banshees only follow certain families in Ireland son…there's the O'Brien's of course, the O'Connor's and the O'Grady's, the O'Neill's and what's the other one Jean?" Ellie asked Mrs. McGrath.

"The Kavanagh's."

"That's it, the Kavanagh's. She comes and wails the night before the soul is to leave the body."

"And do ya know…" said Mrs. McGrath sitting down. "It's said the wailin's so sharp it can shatter glass."

Again they both blessed themselves. Red found all this intriguing and continued with his questions.

"What does she look like?"

"You tell him Ellie, ya know all about the Shees."

"Well now, let's see, she usually appears as an old woman wearin' a grey hooded cape. She has long grey hair that reaches the ground and sits combin' it with a pure silver comb."

"She's also called a 'ban chaointe' in the Irish, which means a keenin' woman. Isn't that right Ellie?"

"That she is. Sure everyone hears a Shee at some stage in their lives and when ya do, it'll send shivers down yer spine."

"What's keenin'?" asked Red.

"It's like, wailin', cryin'. There used to be women years ago that were paid ta wail at funerals and wakes," answered Ellie.

"Sounds a bit weird ta me, paid criers?" laughed Red.

"It's true all right. My grandmother used ta tell me about it," said Mrs. McGrath.

"Somebody was tellin' me that Banshees have different forms they appear in, is that true?" Red asked.

"It is, now I have never heard of one takin' a different form here in this part of the world, but I know they can appear as a hooded crow, a stoat, even a hare or a weasel," replied Mrs. McGrath.

"So if ya hear one, ya know for sure that someone, in one of the families they follow is about to die?" Red asked.
They both made the sign of the cross again and nodded.

On leaving the house Red stopped for a moment in the doorway and thought about what his grandmother and Mrs. McGrath had been saying. Just on an impulse, he decided to take the long way to the town centre and go via Hyde Market. As he approached the O'Brien's house, he noticed a man dressed in black working at the front door. When he got closer, he saw that he was pinning a black crepe cross to the door. This was the sign that someone in the house had passed away.
"Has someone died?" Red asked the man whom he now recognized as a local undertaker.
"Ah indeed. Mrs. O'Brien passed away in her sleep. May the Lord have mercy on her soul."
"She died last night?" Red asked.
"Half past two this very mornin'."
"Sorry ta hear that. Thank you."
'Maybe there's something to this Banshee thing after all,' Red thought as he continued on his way to Hill Street.

When he arrived at Uncle Luigi's, he found Anto, Po, Topcoat and Jumpy standing outside chatting. When all the grunted greetings were finished, Red began telling them the story of the Banshee.
"Jasus that's somethin'," said Jumpy.
"What are ya talkin' about for Christ's sake, sure it's a well known fact that the Shees have been around in Ireland since before we taught the Vikings to play marbles," spouted Topcoat.
"Did ya ever see one?" Jumpy asked Topcoat.
"Naw, never did, but I heard the wailin' a few times for sure."
"What was it like?"
"Scare the shit clean outta ya."
"Jasus."
"It's all auld wives tales," said Anto.
"Don't know about that Anto, ya can't deny the fact that a load of people in our street heard one last night and Mrs. O'Brien died about the same time."

"It was probably some auld stray cat gettin' its oats," laughed Anto.
"Will ya listen ta your man will ya? Sure what would an Italian know about Banshees?" asked Topcoat.
"He would know that it's all a load a shit, that's what he'd know."
"Don't worry yourself Anto, one day you'll hear one, maybe even see one and when ya do, the smile will be on the other side a yer face," snapped Topcoat.
Red felt a tug on the back of his coat.
"Ya left out a family ya know there Red," commented Po.
"Did I, which one?"
"The Fallons."
"Ya could be right there, I think there was another name now that I think of it."
"Yeah, it's the Fallons all right and all the names that come from Fallon."
"What names?" Red played along.
"Let's see, there's the Fallons, the Fallsons, the…holy shit."
"What?"
"Ya know, I think Falsoni would be taken from Fallon."
"Jasus, he's off with the shit again. Ya should be locked up Po for your own safety," laughed Anto.
"Ok, so don't believe me if ya don't want ta. I'll bet ya that some guy called Fallon went over ta Italy and settled there. It's more than likely he ended up bein' called Falsoni."
"That's the biggest load a shit I ever heard," laughed Anto.
"Well, maybe not," intervened Red.
"I heard about an Italian guy that landed in Dublin and they couldn't pronounce his name…what was it now…Lisonie or Lawonie or something and he ended up being called Lewis…and it stuck."
"More shit."
"Naw, its true sure enough Anto."
"Well, anyway…there's no such things as Banshees…it's all auld wives tales."

Later that day Red met up again with Po.
"What was all that about this mornin'?"

"Settin' that frigger up. He's always settin' one of us up, it has ta be near enough his turn by now…huh?"
"You're right ya know, he's always in the middle of somethin' or other… but we've never got around ta settin' him up yet, have we?"
"Now we have ta come up with a plan and it should have somethin' ta do with the Shees."
"Gottya."
"It'll take some plannin' ya know…ta get it right."
"I'll leave that ta your own good wee self Po; you'll come up with a good un."

Three days later Red and Po were sitting on a wall at the back of Red's house on Castle Street.
"Jasus, I've got it!" said Po suddenly.
"Are ya gonna give it ta me?"
"Shut up a minute."
"Ya need help, de ya know that?"
"Shush…let me think."
Po jumped off the wall and paced up and down for a few minutes while Red, chin in hands, watched him.
"Who's that guy in class 3A that's into nature and animals and all that?"
"Pete Harkins?"
"That's him, Pete Harkins. Where does he live?"
"Chapel Street I think."
"Come on."
Red knew when Po had an idea in his head it was best to go along with him. Soon they found themselves walking up Chapel Street. After a couple of inquiries they found Pete Harkins' house easily enough and rapped on the door. Pete himself answered.
"Hi Pete, listen, I heard ya have tapes of animal sounds and stuff?"
"I have loads of animal sounds, which one were ya lookin' for?"
Po rubbed his chin and looked at his feet for a moment.
"Ya know the way a cat cries at night?"
"When it's matin' ya mean?"
"Yeah, I suppose."
"I have that."

"Ya have...brilliant. If I bring ya a tape would ya make a copy for me?"
"Sure, no bother. What do ya want it for anyways?"
"We're planning ta give someone a wee bit of a shock ya might say."

A few days later Po had the tape and borrowed his brother's small tape recorder. Everything was ready. The time selection was now the crucial part.
"Did ya ask your granny this mornin'?" Po asked Red.
"Yeah, nothing really new."
"Why is it that old people are always up ta date on who's sick and dyin'?"
"They're gonna be there soon their own selves I suppose."
"Could be."
"That Mrs. O'Neill on the Ballyholland Road, is still sick though."
"I think we will have ta settle for her now, we can't wait any longer."
"How are ya goin' ta set it up?" asked Red.
"Just the usual. You make sure ya play along with me when I start windin' up Anto."

They were sitting in the first snug in Uncle Luigi's after closing.
"Po...will ya talk about football or sex or somethin' will ya? I'm sick a listenin' ta this shit about Banshees," complained Anto.
"But listen, this is the chance of a lifetime. We might actually get ta hear one, Jasus, maybe even see one," said Po seriously.
"Yeah, right, some chance," laughed Anto.
"How will ya feel tomorra if we go there tonight and hear a Shee and ya didn't come?"
"Oh all right then for Christ's sake, I'll come, but it will be a waste a time."
"Good on ya."
"What time are ya all goin'?"
"It's now half past twelve..." Po looked at his watch.
"About one o'clock would be about right".
"Right, I have ta finish up here, see ya all later," said Anto leaving the snug.
"Well, what's the story then?" asked Red.

"Now ya make an excuse and say ya have ta go home, right? Ya have the recorder and the tape, so ya would need ta head off now. Go to the hedge on the right hand side of the house, ya know, just next ta it and watch for us comin'. We'll get behind the hedge on the other side of the road facin' the house."
"Right, ok, I'll head off now then."
"One more thing, don't go High Street way comin' back in case we run inta ya."
"Right, right."
"I won't see ya till tomorra', I'll call up in the mornin' and tell ya about Anto pissin' himself," laughed Po.
Red made his excuses to Anto and joked with him about hearing a Banshee before he left.

Next morning Red was feeding his grandfather's chickens at the back of his house when he heard Po's voice.
"Yo, ya were a star ya bastard, a star I tell ya. Anto nearly shit."
"What?"
"He nearly had a fit. Shakin' like a leaf he was, all the way home too, never spoke a word."
"What the frig are ya talkin' about Po?"
"Jasus, you're slow in the mornin's Morgan, are ya not wakened up yet?"
"Po, start again…maybe I am a bit slow this mornin'. Now, what are ya talkin' about?"
"Ok, now, ya know your name don't ya?"
Red's clenched fist under Po's chin assured him that he wanted to get on with the conversation.
"Ok, ok…well it worked a treat. When we arrived and settled down behind the hedge, Anto was laughin' and messin'. Then ya switched on the recorder…well holy shit…the wailin' even scared me."
Red looked at Po and scratched his head. He had a puzzled look on his face.
"Po, are we on the same page? Are ya talkin' about Anto and the Shee on the Ballyholland Road last night?"
"For Christ's sake, what else would I be talkin' about?"
"And you and Anto heard it and took off?"

"Took off? That would be one way of puttin' it. Flew would be better. His feet never touched the ground I'm tellin' ya. I never caught up with him until we reached High Street."
Red sat down and looked up at Po.
"Ya better sit down Po."
"What?" said Po sitting.
"Firstly, a went ta the spot we planned. While I was waitin' for you lot I tried out the tape recorder. The whorin' thing wouldn't work. I tried about twenty times, even took out the batteries and put them back, but nothin'. So I just gave up the ghost and went home."
Po thought for a moment and looked directly at Red.
"Now hold on Red, are ya serious? Ya never played the sounds?"
"No."
"At all?"
"No."
"So…what did we hear?"
"I don't know, but it wasn't me."
"Come on," Po jumped up and headed for the back door. Red dutifully followed.
They went into the kitchen and found Red's grandmother cooking.
"Mornin' Mr. Hillen," she smiled.
"Mornin' Mrs. Morgan, listen, is that Mrs. O'Neill up on the Ballyholland Road still sick?"
"Ah poor Jenny O'Neill," she made a sign of the cross. "God took her early this mornin', may she rest in peace."
"She died?"
"That she did."

Po and Red looked at each other.
"Ya know, you boys should get out a lot more instead of sittin' around the house all day. Yous are lookin' very pale ya know."

End

The Success of Failure

1960

"Well, as I remember, it was all Anto's idea," said Po.
"Yeah, a think you're right ya know. It actually was Anto that came up with the whole idea now that a think of it," replied Red.

They were both sitting on top of a large pile of logs at Newry Docks, which afforded them a panoramic view of the harbour and surrounding area. The subject came up about how they managed to get into St. Joseph's Intermediate School. The school had just been built and they were to be its first students.

"Ya remember the meetin' we had down your back yard?" said Po nudging Red with his elbow.
"Jasus, a must be gettin' old, a had forgotten all about that," mused Red.

****

Red's thoughts drifted back in time to the meeting Po had mentioned. It had been called by Anto.

"Right, are we all here?" asked Anto looking around the faces of the gang all seated in a circle on the grass. "So, let's begin. The reason a called ya all here was ta ask ya about the exam we have ta do next week."
"What about it?" asked Red. "A hope you're gonna tell me ya come up with a plan to get the answers?"
"No, in fact the complete opposite," said Anto seriously.
"What do ya mean?" quizzed Po.
Anto took a deep breath. "Do yis remember the past three and a half years? Let me remind yis. Do ya remember the time Lanky Larkin was caught copyin' Naffy McKay's homework by that auld bastard Brother Feenan? He got five slaps on the back of each hand with the edge of a ruler. The welts were there for a week, he could hardly close his hands, and talkin' about Naffy, do yis not remember him bein' caught fightin' in the playground by Brother Warde, him and Jumpy Jones? Both of them got fifteen whacks with the bamboo cane. They were made to bend over the desk, got five on the arse, five on the back of the thighs and five on the back of their lower legs. They could barely walk afterwards."
"Jasus, I remember that, rotten bastard that Brother Warde, what was it ya called him Po?"
"A friggin' whorin' sadist," answered Po with anger in his voice.
"Look, a could go on for the next hour about the beatin's them evil shits gave us since we went ta the Abbey," went on Anto.
"Anto, we all agree that the Christian Brothers are as Christian as the Devil his own self, what are ya gettin' at?" asked Red.
"Right, now yis know there is this new school openin' on the Armagh Road after the Summer Holidays. New classrooms, new gym, new teachers, and, can a point out, it's a Government School. They won't be allowed ta beat us like the 'Black Demons', and most important, none of the friggin' Brothers will be teaching there."
This got a round of applause and cheering.
"Now, have any of ya given any thought ta this? If we pass this stupid exam, we'll have another four years gettin' the shit bate out of us by that crowd of, as Po calls them, sadists, in the Abbey."
"Jasus Anto, de ya know, a never thought a that?" mumbled Po.
"So have ya an idea Anto?" asked Red.

"I have, a very simple one too, we fail."
"What?"
"We fail the exams."
"What do ya mean?" asked Red.
"Well, if we do our best, and pass, it's four more years in hell. If we fail, we get the new school and no Brothers."
"Wow, there's a thought," mused Bishop.
"Sure we'll get hell from the wrinkly crowd if we fail, won't we?" put in Ginger.
"Sure ya will, but ya can always do your next exams from the new place, I asked about that." answered Anto.
"Ya know, I'm for it," said Red holding up his hand.
"Me too," added Po.
"And me," said Bishop.

It was unanimously agreed by all there that the exams should be, at all costs, failed.
"Hey, Jumpy and Dunno aren't here?" noticed Po looking around.
"No need ta worry about them two," laughed Anto. "They'll fail the bit that says, 'Name and Address'."
This got a round of applause and laughter.

The day came for the exams and all the gang took part. When they were over, they met up on the Abbey Football Field.
"Well, how did ya do?" Red asked Po who giggled before answering.
"De ya remember the question in the History Test, 'Who was William Shakespeare'? I put, the army's worst spear thrower'," laughed Po.
"That's a class one," laughed Red. "I had a good one too in the same test, 'Who was Guy Fawkes?' I put, 'A guy that worked for the IRA'," laughed Red.
"Did you have any good ones Anto," asked Po.
"Yeah, a did. It was in the Maths Test. The one about the train. 'If a train travels at 50 miles per hour, how long would it take to travel 175 miles'?"
"What did ya put?" asked Red smiling.
"I just said, 'A good long time'," laughed Anto.

"Ah sure here's the geniuses comin'. Well Jumpy and Dunno, how did yis get on?"
"Jasus it was very hard so it was," replied Jumpy as the two sat down beside the rest of the boys.
"That it was, I couldn't get that one about the train either Anto. What a stupid question, sure I was never on a train for 175 miles, how was I supposed ta know how long it took?"
This got a loud cheer from the gang.

Two months later, on their last day at school, the exam results were published. The boys were amazed to find that they had all failed and would be moving to St. Joseph's Intermediate School after the School Holidays. The gang met up that evening in Uncle Luigi's for celebratory fish and chips.
"Po, tell the lads about your encounter with that whore Feenan," said Red.
"Well, sure I was only walkin' out of the school mindin' my own business when your man, the Black Demon called me. 'Young Hillen,' says he, 'I was very disappointed in your exam results. I felt sure you would have flown through and be with us for another while'."
"What did ya say?" asked Anto.
"I said, 'Sure these things happen Brother. But failure sometimes has a good side to it.' Well, sure he looked at me and says 'Like what?' Well I looked him straight in the face and a says, 'The good side is, I'll never have ta see you again, will a'?"
"Jasus Christ, ya did not?" gasped the Bishop.
"I did, and he says, 'Get out of my sight you impudent brat'. Well I just looked at him again and a says, 'Sure that will be an entire pleasure'."
Po sat back and folded his arms smiling.
"De ya know, I never enjoyed anythin' as much since Red fell in the cow shit."
When the laughter died down, Anto stood up.
"Gentlemen and scholars, fairies, fruits and Jumpy and Dunno, raise your glasses for a toast." Everyone held up their coffees and their Cokes.
"To the rest of our lives without the Black Demons."

****

"That was some time wasn't it," smiled Red.
"That it was, in fact one of Anto's best ever ideas."
"De ya know, you're right it was. Look at the crack we're havin' now at St. Joes, imagine being still stuck in the Abbey? I'm sure glad I failed that exam," laughed Red.
"Correct and right, a total success. Hey, sure that's what it was now that a think of it."
"What?" asked Red.
"The 'Success of Failure'," laughed Po.

End

Liar's Ice Cream

1959

"Hi Red, Anto," said Jammy sliding into the snug.
"Hi Jammy, what's happenin'?" asked Anto.
"Nothin' much, saw Po last night out Ashgrove when I was with my uncle in the car."
"Hang on, ya saw Po out Ashgrove?" asked Red.
"Yeah."
"Who was with him?" interrupted Anto.
"Your wee one from High Street, Jasus, what's her name, Marie somethin'."
"Marie Chambers?" asked Red.
"That's her, dark curly hair, great legs, yeah, that's her."
Red and Anto looked at each other.
"Now, a wonder why that wee shit never told us he had a date with Marie Chambers?" asked Anto.
"Why indeed, why did he not want us ta know he was goin' out with her?" mused Red.
"He's up ta somethin' so he is. Jammy, if ya happen ta run into that wee shit, don't tell him ya were talkin' ta us, ok?" said Anto.
"No problem."

Jammy left a few minutes later.
"Now what do ya make of this then?" asked Anto.
"Ya know, now that a think about it, he was out with Marian the other night, went to the Pictures," said Red.
"Yeah, he brought her back here afterwards, I remember. He's been out with her quite a few times, I was of the opinion he was goin' steady with her."
"He is, at least that's what he told me anyway," answered Red.
"I see. Well now, the wee frigger's been caught two timin' so he has," smiled Anto.
"Indeed he has. My God, we actually have somethin' on Po, I can't believe it," laughed Red.
"He said he would be in later tonight, at closin', make sure you're here. I'm dyin' to hear what he has ta say," smiled Anto.
"So am I."

Later that night Red was sitting in the front snug with Anto, Topcoat, Jumpy and Bishop.
They were all told about Po's exploits on the romance field.
"Now not a word out of any of ya, right?" said Anto pointing his finger around the group.

Po eventually arrived.
"Well girls," he smiled as he squeezed into the snug.
"Would ya look what the cat dragged in," smiled Red.
"Well, sir, and how's life been with ya?" asked Anto.
"Nothin' excitin', borin' in fact."
"Did he say, borin'?" Anto asked Red.
"I could swear that's just what he said all right," said Red seriously.
"Borin' indeed, and sure you with a beautiful sexy girlfriend that ya can take out anytime," went on Anto.
"Yeah, a know, with my looks ya see, I'm able ta get the best ya know. Sure Marian's just crazy about me," said Po leaning back and looking at the ceiling.
"Really, crazy about ya is she?" asked Red.
"Well, as ya know, I'm not one ta boast," smiled Po.

"Crazy about ya is she indeed. So you have a sort of open relationship then have ya?" asked Anto.

"Open, what do ya mean?"

"Open, like she can go out with other fellas if she likes?" continued Anto.

"That's an odd thing ta say, why would ya ask that?"

"You tell him Red."

"Well, it's just that Marian, sorry, your Marian, was seen out with Billy Makin last night."

"That's a total lie so it is," said Po.

"A total lie is it?" asked Anto.

"Yis it is," snapped Po.

"Well a have ta tell ya Po, I am for one, glad ta hear it so a am. All this two timin' that goes on nowadays, a can't have it ya know."

"I would agree with Red, what about you guys?" Anto asked the rest of the company.

"Bad news so it is," said Topcoat. "Makes people out ta be dishonest so it does, sneaky too."

"I would agree with that 100%," said Red.

"Well then, so Marian was not out with your man Billy Makin then?" Anto asked Po.

"No she wasn't. Marian wouldn't do that," replied Po.

"But Po, now just talkin' hypothetically now, great word that Anto isn't it?"

"Bloody is, makes ya sound very posh."

"I am very posh. Now, back ta Marian. Now Po, as a said, just speakin' hypothetically, how would ya know if Marian was out with Billy Makin or not?"

"Cause as it happens she was with me last night."

"Ah, she was with him last night," said Red to Anto.

"Well then, sure she could not be in two places at the same time then could she?" answered Anto. There was general agreement around the table.

"Now do ya know, that's a bit weird so it is," commented Red.

"What is?" asked Anto.

"I was only talkin' ta Marian yesterday and she said she wasn't goin' out last night."

"Did she say that Red?" said Anto.
"Her very words."
"Jasus."
"Said she was havin' an early night, washin' her hair and stuff like women do."
"Now isn't that somethin'," said Anto seriously.
"What are yous friggers up ta?" asked Po looking at Red.
"Us? Why Po, we're not up ta anything. Just wonderin' why you and Marian have two different stories?"
"How do I know, just a mix up, that's all," said Po, his face getting a little red.
"Now Red, de ya know, we were sayin' earlier that it's bad news ta two time and lie about it, but de ya know what's even worse?"
"Tell me," said Red.
"Tellin' lies ta your best friends and pals and people that stand by ya and care for ya."
"Ya have never spoken truer words Anto," said Red with passion.
"All right, all right for frig sake, so I went for a walk with Marie Chambers, so what?"
There was a combined burst of laughter from all in the snug followed by a round of applause. When things settled down Anto was first to speak.
"I don't suppose ya know the penalty for tellin' lies ta your mates here in Uncle Luigi's do ya Po?"
"What?"
"Ya get Ice Cream."
"I get Ice Cream?"
"Ya do."
"Jasus, I'll tell lies more often so a will," smiled Po.
"I'll go and get it for ya," said Anto leaving the snug.
A few moments later he was back with a very large scoop of Ice Cream.
"Grab him," smiled Anto.
Po was unceremoniously dragged from the snug and onto the floor. His hands and feet were firmly held while Anto opened his trousers and poured the Ice Cream down the front of his underpants to the screams and protests of Po. He then re buttoned Po's trousers and patted Po's

groin area to make sure the Ice Cream was well bedded in. Po was now allowed to stand which he did very slowly.
“Ahhh, yis bastardin’, whorin’ friggin’ shitheads.”
“Sure I’m awful sorry Po but sure it’s the law of the house that ya get, ‘Liar’s Ice Cream’.”
This got a sustained round of applause followed by much swearing, moaning, complaining and grumbling from Po.

End

Heavenly Revenge

1959

"At the end of the day we were lucky to get a draw," said Red.
"Suppose so, considerin' we were playin' hatchet men," snarled Po.
"Correct and right, all they seemed ta be interested in was hackin' our players down and that bloody referee could see nothin' wrong, stupid blind bastard."
"Poor Ginger, they say his ankle is cracked, he will be out for a few months for sure."
"And that whorin' referee never even gave a foul for that tackle either," complained Red.

The two boys were walking along North Street discussing the football match between Castle Street Rangers and Dromalane, who were to say the least, bitter rivals in the Newry Summer League.

"Do ya know, every Friday when a go down our back yard a get angry when a see them buggers' shirts hangin' out," said Red.
"What buggers' shirts?"
"Dromalane of course."

"Hold on, Dromalane football shirts? Hanging on a line on Castle Street?" asked Po.
"Yeah, Mrs. whatsherface, McDonald, ya know, Limpy McDonald, the Dromalane Manager, that's her brother. She washes the kit for them every week."
"Holy Jasus, Dromalane shirts hanging in Castle Street, a disgrace so it is, but…?"
"But what?"
"Time for a little pay back maybe?" smiled Po.
"Jasus, he's off again. What are ya up ta now?"
"Not sure, but a think I might be gettin' an idea. Tell me about Mrs. McDonald, ya say she washes the shirts every Friday and hangs them out in the afternoon ta dry?"
"Like clockwork. Hangs them out just after one o'clock, then ten minutes later she passes our house on her way ta do her shoppin'."
"Excellent."
"What is?"
"Will ya wait? Now, this Friday, we are goin' ta give her a wee nasty surprise. I got the idea from ma mom," said Po wearing a broad grin.
"Will ya tell me?" asked Red impatiently.
"De ya know what, you are the most impatient person I have ever met in my entire life."
"Tell me ya wee creep."
"I will, I will, later. Now, I have ta see a few of the lads, so, we meet here on Friday at exactly one o'clock, right?"
"Suppose."

Friday arrived, and seated on a wall in Red's back yard were, Bishop, Jumpy, Topcoat, Po and Red. All were holding on to small bags.
"There she is," said the Bishop pointing across the gardens.
Mrs. Mc Donald had arrived in her back yard and was hanging out the Dromalane football kit. Around ten minutes later, the job was completed, 12 football shirts, 12 football shorts and 12 pairs of football socks.
"Now we give her about 15 minutes, right? Then we go," smiled Po. "Red you go up to your house and watch for her passin'." Red disappeared at speed back up the garden to his house. He waited

at the window in his hallway until he saw Mrs. McDonald passing with her shopping bags. He returned quickly to the boys and informed them that she had left her house.
"Right now lads, let's go, and no noise."
All five set off across the three gardens separating Red's and Mrs. McDonald's. When they arrived Po gathered them around.
"Right now lads, watch," said Po as he approached the clothesline. He made a gurgling sound and spat on one of the shirts.
"That's for Ginger," said Po.
The Bishop moved forward and spat on another shirt.
"And that's just for bein' a bunch a bastards."
Red followed suit.
"That's for tryin' ta injure me last week."
Topcoat spat on one of the shirts.
"That's for not bein' sportsmen."
Jumpy was last and had to think.
"Go on will ya Jumpy?" encouraged Po.
"What'll a say?"
"Anythin' ya friggin' want ta, will ya hurry up."
Jumpy stood for a moment, then marched forward and spat on a shirt.
"That's for bein' from Dromalane."
"Jasus," moaned Bishop. "May the Lord save me from the Jumpy's of this world."
"Save us all," added Red laughing.
"Right now lads, get ta work, spread it well around, and quickly."
The bags, which contained bread crumbs and stale bread, were emptied around the area under the clothes line.

Twenty minutes later the boys were sitting in Red's back garden.
"Look, look," said Topcoat, "another three pigeons arrived."
"There's Crows, Starlings, Pigeons, and even Blackbirds," smiled Bishop.
"Don't forget the Redbreasts, Tits and Greys," added Red.

A week later Red and Po were sitting in Uncle Luigi's when 'Silly' Crilly walked in. He was the Dromalane Goalkeeper.

"Silly, I heard a weird thing, that yous guys had ta play in damp shirts last week, is that true?"
"It's true all right. Mrs. Mc Donald washes our kit so she does. She put it out last week ta dry so she did and when she came back the whole kit was covered in bird shit and she had ta wash it again. It wasn't dry in time for the match so it wasn't."
"Jasus, sure that's awful Silly. Same thing happened to my mom with her washin'. Our wee fella threw out some bread and the birds flew down and shit all over her washin'."

When Silly had left, Po held up his Coke bottle and clinked Red's.
"That was what ya might call, sweet revenge, droppin's from on high," smiled Po.
"Ya know, a think I would call it 'Heavenly Revenge'," smiled Red.

End

A Goat Called Willie

1960

Red Morgan's grandfather had a goat called Willie. This was no ordinary goat according to Red. He explained to Po that Willie was unusually intelligent for a goat and understood almost everything said to him. The two boys were sitting on a wall in the back garden of Red's house on Castle Street watching Willie graze.

"Well, he doesn't look very smart ta me," said Po, chin in hands studying an unconcerned Willie.

"But ya don't know him. Ya would need ta spend time with him ta get ta know his ways," explained Red who was sitting in the same pose as Po.

"Well, ask him a question then," suggested Po.

"Ask him what?"

"Jasus, I don't know, just ask him a question."

Red thought for a moment.

"Hi, Willie."

Willie looked up at Red.

"What would ya think about goin' ta school?"

Willie went back to grazing.

"There ya are, no response, he doesn't know what the hell ya'r sayin'," laughed Po.
"Don't be stupid Po, of course he does, sure didn't he just answer me."
"What are ye talkin' about?"
"He went back to eating grass, didn't he?"
"So?"
"That's his way of sayin' he doesn't give a shit about school. He just ignored the question."
"Jasus Morgan, ya talk some crap so ya do."
"So, don't believe me then."
"I don't."
"Good."
"Good."
"Ya know, I might have an idea here for a bit of fun with the lads," mused Red.
"What?"
"Well, how does this sound…?" Red moved his head closer to Po and continued the conversation in conspiratorial whispers.

Later that day, the two boys were at the Abbey football field with most of the gang.
"…and Red claims that Willie is really smart," Po was explaining to the listening group.
"Maybe he is," suggested Jumpy.
"Don't you start Jumpy, one nutter in the gang's enough."
"But why do ya think he's smart Red?" asked Kitter.
"Because I know him and I can ask him a question and he'll answer me."
"You're sayin' ya have a smart goat Red?" asked Anto.
"That he is."
"So we can put him to the test then?"
"Maybe."
"What de ya mean…maybe?" asked Anto.
"Well, I don't want him put under pressure, otherwise he'll do nothin'."
"Ok then, so we are allowed to ask him one question then?" put in Kitter.

"That would be ok I suppose," answered Red.
"But how would he answer, I mean, he can't talk can he?"
"Good point," said the up to now quiet Po.
"I suggest we simply ask him ta do somethin'."
"Sounds good ta me," said Anto. A murmur of general agreement followed.

Later that afternoon the gang had all gathered in Red's back garden.
"Now, this is the plan. We'll ask Willie to do somethin'."
"What?" asked Anto.
"Well…let's see, he's locked up in his house at the moment and I have to feed him. Now ya know what goats are like, they'll eat anythin', right?"
"Right," they all answered.
"So we pick a piece of food and tell Willie to go and eat it."
"Aw no ya don't…the food ya pick might be his favourite so he would go to it anyway," said Po.
"Good point Po," said Red. "We'll do it scientifically right? So this is what we'll do, we'll let him out, as ya say, he'll go to his favourite food, then we will put him in again. When we let him out the second time we will tell him to go to another piece of food."
"That sounds like a good idea, let's do it," added Anto.

Red laid out some vegetables, fruit and bread for Willie in a line.
"Now his favourite is apples, right?"
Red opened the door to Willie's house and let him out. He headed straight for the apple.
Red then took him by the collar and put him back in his house.
"Ok, so we now know for sure that Willie loves apples."
All agreed.
"This time, even though there are apples there, I will tell him to have a piece of bread."
Again, all agreed.
Red rearranged the food in a line in front of Willie's house, adding another piece of bread un-noticed by the gang. He opened the door and while holding Willie by the collar, told him to have a piece of bread. The bread had been placed at the very end of the line of food,

furthest away from Willie. He released Willie who, lo and behold, went straight for the bread. This prompted a round of applause from all present.

From that day forward Willie became known as Newry's smartest goat and wore a handmade badge on his collar stating that fact.

The test had been done fairly and squarely…well almost. The only small fact that Red and Po had withheld was that the bread in question was soaked in pure apple juice for three hours before the test. It seemed too petty to mention!

Another Day in the Life of 3C

1960

The infamous 3C were now into their last year at school to the great relief of all the teaching staff. They were now in a new term, a new year, but alas, no change in the trouble and mayhem this one class could cause.

(1) The History Class

"Right now 3C, settle down," roared Mr. Sweeney.
Peter Sweeney was a tall, well built, but rather untidy man in his early forties. His tie was never straight, his trousers never quite pulled up fully and his black curly hair never seemed to sit the way it was supposed to.
"Let's see now…today we are going to start on a new chapter in history, the War of the Roses."
"Where was this, Sir?" asked Bishop Keenan.
"The wars took place in medieval England from 1455 to 1487."
"And they fought with flowers, Sir?" asked Red.

"No! Now don't start being silly Morgan."

"But you just said they were the Wars of the Roses, Sir," added Blackie.

"There was a daisy shortage," piped up Kitter.

"Murray, shut up! That was the name given to the wars because of the badges worn by the combatants."

"They wore badges, Sir, the combat…people?" asked Jumpy.

"Combatants."

"That's them Sir, they wore badges?"

"Yes Jones, they wore badges. The House of York for example…they wore a white rose badge and…"

"The wars were between two houses Sir?" asked Red.

"Yes Morgan, the House of Lancaster and the House of York."

"So they were just wee wars then Sir?"

"What are you talking about Morgan?"

"I thought they were like real wars, ya know, like with thousands of soldiers fighting with swords and knives and spears…"

"Bows and arrows, don't forget the bows and arrows," added Dunno.

"Look, settle down now 3C. Yes there were thousands of soldiers fighting…"

"Now that's what ya call a house," said Jumpy.

"What Jones?"

"All them thousands of soldiers…and don't forget their families…all livin' in one house. That must a been some house."

"No Jones, you have the wrong idea…you see…"

"They didn't live in houses, Sir?"

"They did of course but…"

"That's terrible, isn't it Red?" said Kitter.

"All them soldiers with the nice badges all crushed together in a wee house."

"Was there a housin' shortage Sir?"

"Quiet!" roared Mr. Sweeney. 3C was silent.

"Now I'm not going to have any nonsense in this class…do you understand?"

"Yes Sir," 3C replied in one voice.

"Now…let's move along."

"Sir?"

"Yes McAteer."
"I didn't hear ya right Sir. Did ya say there would be no sense in the class Sir?"
"No McAteer, I said there would be, no nonsense."
"Oh, right Sir, sorry about that."
"Now let's get on. The War of the Roses lasted, as you can see from the dates, almost thirty two years."
"That was a very long war so it was Sir," helped Dunno.
"Yes it was McManus, in those days that would have been normal."
"But Sir, like if you joined the army when you were say, thirty five, by the time ya could go home again ya would have been an auld fella."
"Well, that in a way was the case, but very few soldiers lasted more than three years in those days. The death rate was very high due to the way they fought battles you see, now for example..."
"Sir?"
"Yes McAteer."
"That doesn't make a lot of sense ta me Sir. Sure if ya knew ya would be knocked off within three years, ya'd be a right ejit to join the army in the first place."
"I agree with Jammy Sir," put in Red. "It would be a good way ta commit suicide so it would."
"Them English were all mad in the first place. Fightin' over flowers, livin' in wee houses, wearin' fancy badges and joinin' up in the army ta get themselves killed over it all," commented Dunno.
"Look, 3C, just open your text books at page thirty and begin reading from there. I have urgent things to read in this newspaper, so get on with it."
"Red, I don't think Mr. Sweeney likes us," said Jammy.
"I think you're not wrong," answered Red.
"McAteer, Morgan, heads down and get on with it."
"Terrible when people don't like ya," mumbled Jammy almost to himself.

****

(2) The English Class

Through a clatter of desk tops, shuffling feet, laughing, talking, shouting, Mr. Gray was aware that 3C had arrived in his classroom. He was a thin, fair haired man with rimless glasses resting precariously on a long narrow pointed nose. A neat little man was John Gray, who always wore the same tweed jacket and dark trousers.

"Now 3C, settle down and pay attention," demanded Mr. Gray.
3C did make an effort one has to say, all be it a poor one.
"Today we are going to do some work on your writing skills."
"Can't do that Sir," said Jumpy.
"And pray, tell me why not Jones?"
"I don't have any writin' skills Sir."
"Jones, it's simply a figure of speech."
"Speech has figures Sir?" asked Jammy.
"Don't start being silly now McAteer, it's simply…"
"But ya just said that, ya said speech had a figure Sir."
"I heard that too," added Red.
"You are not going to distract me with your stupidity 3C, so you can stop now," smiled Mr. Gray.
"So get your copy books out and write down the following exactly as it is on the blackboard."
Mr. Gray wrote the sentence, 'In summertime the flowers are in bloom.'
There was a few moments silence throughout the class.
"Sir?"
"Yes Morgan," said Mr. Gray beginning to feel a tiredness creeping in.
"Not all flowers bloom in the summer Sir."
"So what Morgan?"
"Then that there sentence is wrong Sir."
"Morgan, it's just simply a sentence for writing practice, it does not have to be factual."
"But then Sir, sure ya'r gettin' us ta write down lies," put in Jammy.
"That doesn't seem right a'tall," added Bishop speaking up for the first time.
"All right, all right," shouted Mr. Gray, who was at this time beginning to feel his temperature rising dramatically. "I'll change it for you."

Mr. Gray rubbed out the sentence and started again. This time he wrote, 'In summertime, some flowers are in bloom.'
"Right now 3C, copy this down, please."
"Sir, that's not right either," said Red.
Mr. Gray sat down slowly at his desk.
"What is wrong with it now Morgan?"
"Well Sir, if they were flowers, they would be already in bloom wouldn't they? Like up to when they bloom they are just plants, then they become flowers. De ya know what a mean Sir?"
Mr. Gray lowered his head into his hands.
"Red's right Sir, if ya look at a plant that has no flowers ya just call it a plant so ya do. But if it has petals then ya all would call it a flower," explained Dunno.
Mr. Gray looked up at 3C, looked at his watch again and took another deep breath.
"I want you to write the following sentence in your copy books, in your very best handwriting. 'I must not antagonise Mr. Gray'," he said very slowly.
"Sir?"
"Yes Morgan."
"How do ya spell antagmise?"
Mr. Gray rose slowly.
"Open your text books and read chapter one, very quietly please until I come back."
Mr. Gray left the classroom. He needed his pills.

****

(3) The Religious Education Class

As 3C eventually got themselves seated, Mr. Reed took a deep breath to try and settle himself for what he knew would be a battle of wits. Thomas Reed was at one time, it was rumoured, in a Seminary, training to be a priest. He was a quiet, inoffensive man, almost too quiet one would think to be a teacher. Dressed usually in a dark suit, he looked more like a bank official.
"Now today 3C we are going to talk about the Son of God. Now what can you tell me about Jesus Christ?"

A number of hands went into the air.
"Yes…ah...Jones."
"He was a Jew Sir," spurted out Jumpy.
"Well, yes He was…"
"So does that mean we're Jews too?" asked Red sensibly.
"No it does not Morgan, we are first of all Christians and then..."
"But Sir, if Jesus was born a Jew, lived His whole life as a Jew and died a Jew…and we follow His teachings then we must be Jews...a mean He never said He had given up being a Jew."
"No…I see your point but you don't understand..."
"Sir if Jesus died a Jew, when did He turn a Catholic? Did they make Him a Catholic after He died?" asked Bishop.
"No…I mean…yes…Christendom was…"
"Sir, when Christ died all His followers started the Christians and made Him the head of the Church and put in His resignation to the Jews," explained Jumpy Jones. He looked across to Red.
"There ya see, I know all about it so I do."
"No, not exactly Jones…you see it's..."
"Sir…look…is it true or not, that Jesus never gave up being a Jew?"
"Yes, Christ died, I suppose, still a member of the Jewish faith, but…"
"Now I get it, so Father Meed is really our Rabbi then?" put in Bishop.
"Don't start being silly now Keenan…Now we will move on to…"
"Sir, but ya told us the other week that the Pope came in a direct line from Peter, who was Christ's main man, who was a Jew too," said Red.
"Yes, so what's your point Morgan?"
"Well, then sure the Pope would be a Jew then."
"No, you have it all wrong, look, we will deal with this point at another time. We will move on to the saints now and make a start. Now let's see…" Mr. Reed nervously flipped the pages of the book on his desk.
"Right now, we will start with Joan of Arc, what can anyone tell me about her?"
"Sir, Sir," shouted Jumpy.
"Yes, Jones."
"She was the wife of Noah," he blurted out.

The class burst into laughter. Even Mr. Reed had to turn away to hide a stifled laugh.

Mr. Reed looked at his watch again. Only another thirty minutes. 'I should have taken my father's advice and become a plumber,' he thought.

****

(4) The Art Class

Mr. John Courtney sat at his desk in the Art Classroom staring at his class schedule. *Thursday, 2.00pm, 3C.* 'Not a nice way to end a Thursday afternoon' he thought, 'and it was such a good day too.' Just then the door burst open and an explosion of noise alerted Mr. Courtney that 3C had arrived.

"Quiet 3C, sit down at your desks quietly please."
After a few minutes the noise seemed to have abated somewhat and Mr. Courtney could almost hear himself think.
"Jones, Keenan, hand out these papers, just one sheet each. The rest of you get your water jars, brushes and paints from the desk over there."

Five minutes later, 3C were settled again and Mr. Courtney cleared his throat.
"Now today we are going to paint an Irish cottage in the countryside with the mountains in the background. Add trees, flowers, and plenty of colour, begin."
"What sort of house Sir?" asked Lanky Larkin.
"An Irish cottage Larkin, with a thatched roof and flowers in the garden."
"We have ta paint a garden too?" asked Jumpy Jones.
"And mountains," added Red Morgan.
"And fields," put in Bishop Keenan.
"Don't forget the trees, I like trees," said Dunno McManus.
"What time of year is it Sir?" asked Red.
"It doesn't matter what time of year Morgan, just paint," growled Mr. Courtney.

"But the time of year is very important Sir, like sure the flowers would be all different in winter than they would be in summer."
"Red's right Sir, if it was winter the trees would have no leaves so they wouldn't," added Jumpy.
"And sure there might be snow on the mountains too," said Ginger McVerry.
Mr. Courtney took a deep breath as if to calm himself.
"Decide whatever season you like, summer, winter, spring, autumn, whatever you like, just do it."
"I'm goin' ta do winter, but I'll need more blue so a will," said Jumpy.
"Why will you need more blue Jones," asked Mr. Courtney innocently.
"Ach Sir, winter Sir, it will be cold and in the cold everything goes blue."
"I must have done something very bad in a previous life," Mr. Courtney mumbled to himself.
"You had a previous life sir?" asked Red.
"No, no, just get on with your work Morgan."
"My grandda says he was a Viking warrior in a previous life," said Dunno loudly.
"Sure your grandda only has one leg, how could he have been a Viking warrior dopey," said Jumpy.
This got a ripple of laughter throughout the class.
"Don't be stupid, sure in a previous life he would've had two legs for God's sake," answered Dunno angrily.
"How do ya know he would've had two legs, does he have a photo or somethin'?"
"Vikin's didn't have cameras ya auld ejit," laughed Jumpy.
"Well then how would he know?"
"They did paintin's then so they did," commented Red.
"On the subject of painting, gentlemen and Vikings, can you get on with your work please, now," came the loud voice of Mr. Courtney.
"Oh!" came a shout from the back of the class.
"McVerry, what are you doing?"
"Nothing Sir."
"Why is your face covered in paint?"
"It was a total accident Sir," pleaded Boots Markey.

"An accident?"
"Yes Sir, totally. I had a cramp in ma arm and was stretching it when Ginger's face got in the way."
"Go and clean your face McVerry and I do not want to hear any more disturbances, is that clear, all of you?"
"Yes Sir," came the united reply from 3C.

Mr. Courtney was now walking around the class glancing at the work being done. He stopped beside Boots Markey.
"What is that Markey?" said Mr. Courtney pointing at Boots painting.
"That's grass Sir."
"Blue grass?"
"Yes Sir."
"Blue grass, I see. I won't ask," said Mr. Courtney as he walked on. He stopped beside Dunno.
"And what is that covering half the page?"
"A wall Sir."
"A wall? All that can be seen is the roof of the house McManus."
"But ya see Sir, out where I live the walls are very high."
"I see, I knew it was a mistake to ask."
"Keenan, why is the back of your head green?" asked Mr. Courtney approaching Keenan's desk quickly.
"Is it Sir?"
"Did you do that Roberts?"
"I couldn't see Sir so a couldn't," pleaded Boney Roberts.
"You couldn't see?"
"No Sir."
"I know I will regret this but, why could you not see Roberts?"
"Well Sir, ya see, Bishop has Brylcreem on his hair Sir. The sun was shinin' on it and sure a couldn't see ma paintin'. So a put a wee bit of paint on it ta take the shine away."
"I knew I should not have asked. The sad thing is, it almost makes sense to me, I am getting too old for this job. Keenan, go to the bathroom and wash that paint out of your hair, and quickly."
"Sir?"
"Yes Morgan?" sighed Mr. Courtney.

"Does this Irish Cottage have one or two floors?"
"Just the ground floor Morgan. People could not afford two floors in those days. Plus it made the inside easier to heat in winter."
"There mustn't have been much room Sir with the whole family and the cats and dogs."
"Interesting point Morgan. Most farmers also had some of their animals inside, but not the cats and dogs."
"Why not the cats and dogs?"
"They slept on the roof which was warm from the fire. Sometimes if there were too many of them they fell through the thatch, hence the saying, 'Raining cats and dogs'."
"There must have been some smell inside with all the animals for sure," said Jumpy.
"Just like your house," laughed Dunno.
Jumpy's paint brush found its way into the laughing Dunno's ear.
"Right stop the messing and get on with your work," roared Mr. Courtney.

Near the end of the class Mr. Courtney looked at his watch and a distinctive sigh of relief could be heard through a barely perceptible smile.
"McAteer, collect all the water jars. McManus, collect the paint and brushes."
The noise level rose immediately.
"Quiet 3C."
There was a loud crash at the back of the class followed by swearing and groans.
"What's going on back there McAteer?"
Jammy was standing with his mouth open staring at the students around him. Mr. Courtney hurried to the back of the class where he discovered around six students sitting soaked in various shades of water.
"What happened here?" asked a shocked Mr. Courtney.
"Somebody tripped me Sir so they did, and all the water spilled Sir."
"I was celebrating the end of class too soon, I should have known better," moaned Mr. Courtney. "Everyone get rags and get this mess

cleaned up. You lot with paint on you go to the bathroom and get cleaned, move!"

And so another interesting and eventful day ended for 3C's art teacher Mr. Courtney, yet there was still a bright side to it all. It would be a full week before he would see 3C again.

End

The Funeral Offering

1960

Po and Red were walking along Boat Street on their way to serve at a Funeral Mass in the Old Chapel at St. Mary's Graveyard.
"Well I was told he was very well off," mumbled Po.
"I heard that too, so maybe it'll top £200," said Red.
"I think it'll easily pass that."
"What's the story on the bettin'?"
"I haven't heard anythin', no doubt they'll all be waitin' for us on the way home."
"Well Anto says he has taken in nearly £10 already."
"Jasus! By the way, I might have a surprise for ya later," smiled Po.
"What surprise?"
"If I tell ya it won't be a surprise will it?"
"It'd better not be a bad surprise."
"Don't worry, if it comes off ya'll be delighted."
"Ok then."
"Who's sayin' Mass?"
"Your man, shit, what's his name, from Donegal?"
"Oh yeah, the new guy, Father Docherty."
"Him, yeah."

The two arrived at the church and were quickly inside the vestry and dressed.
Father Docherty arrived ten minutes later.
"Good morning lads."
"Mornin' Father."
"Lovely morning, isn't it?"
"Yes Father."
"Is it just the two of you then this morning?"
"Yes Father."
"Who's this…ah…John Daly?" he said reading from his notes.
"Lived up Church Street Father," said Po.
"Did you know him?"
"Didn't know him personally Father. He raced pigeons as far as I know and was pretty well known around the country for it. He won a big race last year; it was all over the papers here."
"Did he indeed, excellent," said Father Docherty making notes.
The door was knocked and in walked Tom Connelly the church caretaker.
"They're here Father."
"Right Tom, be right there."

Father Docherty donned his robes quickly and when ready led the small procession to the entrance gate of the cemetery. Red carried the Holy Water and sprinkler in a silver bucket. Outside, the coffin of John Daly was resting on the shoulders of two of his sons and two of his brothers. The coffin was not allowed to cross the threshold of the graveyard onto consecrated ground, until it had been blessed by a priest. Father Docherty said some prayers in Latin, took the sprinkler and splashed Holy Water on the coffin. He then turned and began the short trek back to the church. The procession ended with the coffin being laid on top of two trestles in front of the Altar. The caretaker had located one of the deceased's sons, Peter, and brought him into the vestry to meet Father Docherty. After shaking hands and making his condolences, Father Docherty began questioning him about his father's life; what type of man he was, what his hobbies were and all the time taking notes. During the Mass Father Docherty gave a beautiful oration on the life of John Daly. The congregation was in no doubt

that old Johnny was well known to this priest. When the Mass reached a certain point, it was Red's job to place the 'collection book' on the lectern just inside the altar gate.
"We will now take up the offering," said Father Docherty.

Traditionally, the nearest male relative of the deceased would walk up to the altar gate, whisper his name and hand the priest money. The priest would then enter his name in the book and read out to the congregation what he had written. Father Docherty reached out and took the first offering from Peter Daly, the dead man's brother.
"Peter Daly…five pounds," said Father Docherty in a loud voice.
This continued through the male relatives, followed by the females and lastly, friends. When the offering was finished, the money was then taken to the vestry by Po to be counted. The Mass then continued to its conclusion. Before the end the priest was handed a note by the church caretaker. He read its contents and related them to the congregation.
"The offering this morning raised the total of £291.14s."
At this point the coffin was lifted onto the shoulders of relatives and carried to the graveside. The procession was passing through the doorway of the church when Red noticed Jumpy being slipped a note by Po. Red caught Po's eye and asked what was going on through facial expression. Po answered that he would tell him later, also using facial expression.

After the coffin was brought to the graveside, a decade of the Rosary said, and final words read out by the priest, the coffin was interred. Red and Po returned to the vestry to take off their cassocks and surpluses. The caretaker came in and handed each of them an envelope. Inside they found the sum of five shillings. This traditional offering was left for them by the relatives of the deceased.
The boys made their way down Chapel Street and continued on until they reached the corner of William Street, where they found a number of men standing.
"Well young Hillen, how much was lifted?"
"£291.14s," answered Po.

"Jasus, I knew it would be a big one," said one of the men. Murmurs of agreement followed from his companions. Red and Po walked on until they reached Uncle Luigi's where they found Jumpy and some of the lads outside chatting. Red picked up on a silent question from Po to Jumpy and a nod in return. Jumpy disappeared as Red and Po went inside where they found an empty snug and ordered Cokes.

"Well, are ya gonna tell me now?" asked Red.

"What?"

"The surprise."

"Oh, that, in about ten minutes," answered Po looking at his watch.

At this point Anto arrived and slid into the snug beside Red.

"Well, what was the total?"

Po told him. Anto started going through a notebook and mumbling to himself.

"Ah, not great, just made a couple of bob, see ya later," Anto went back to work.

"Ya know, when ya think about it; they collect some great money for the dead man's family, don't they?" said Po.

"What are ya talkin' about?"

"The money they collect at the Mass. They make a lot for the family don't they? I think it's a great idea."

"Po, ya haven't a clue have ya?"

"What?" enquired Po.

"That money's not for the dead man's family dopey."

"Of course it is."

"No it's not. I only found that out a few months ago. The money goes to the priests," explained Red.

"You're shitin' me."

"Swear to God, that's where it goes. It's divided up between them."

"If that's true, then why do the people give so much, ya know for sure most of them can't afford it."

"It's a sort of prestige thing, ya know? The more money collected the more important the deceased was in life."

"Yeah, I see what ya mean. Sure that's friggin' almost blackmail!"

"Yep, that it is, but very clever, isn't it?" smirked Red.

"Well," said a breathless Jumpy as he arrived at the snug.
He handed Po an envelope. Po checked inside, took out some money and handed it to Jumpy who smiled and left without a word.
"What's this?"
"Shush, I'm countin'."
Po then handed Red fifteen shillings. Red's eyes opened wide.
"Jasus, what's this?"
"Your surprise."
"What?"
"Ok, this is the way it went down. Jumpy came up ta the graveyard."
"Yeah, I know."
"I gave him a note telling him how much was collected. Well, he cut over the rocks ta Church Street and was in time to get a bet on with Macko Robinson. He was givin' 3 – 1 for the person who got the nearest amount to what was collected at the Mass. I got Jumpy to put on ten bob, five for you and five for me. I gave the total as £291.10s, so I was only four bob out. I couldn't give the exact amount, it would have looked too suspicious."
"Ya crafty wee shit."
"Believe it."
Red just shook his head, smiled and held up his Coke bottle.
"Ya know, maybe I'll become a priest."
"What?" came Po's shocked response.
"It's the best paid job in Newry when ya think about it."
"What are ya talkin' about?"
"Well, ya see, when you're born your parents pay the priest ta Baptise ya, right?"
"Right."
"Then, when you're growin' up, ya get sick or break a leg or somethin', your parents pay the priest ta pray for ya."
"They do, don't they?"
"Wait, I'm not finished yet. Then, ya decide ta get married, ya pay the priest. Ya have kids, ya pay the priest. It's a continuous circle."
"Wow, never thought of it like that," mused Po rubbing his chin.

"And, still they're not finished with ya. When ya die, your family pay the priest for the mass he says at the Old Chapel and he then goes and takes up the Offering which is divided between them. Then, ya would think, that's that...no way. Now your family comes along and pays the priest to say masses for ya and ta pray for your soul...forever."
"Jasus...where do we get the forms ta sign up?" said Po quickly.
Red laughed.
"Well, here's to a few bob the priests will never get."
"Amen my son."

End

Pitch and Toss

1960

It was a grey, overcast Sunday morning, as Red, Po, and Jumpy passed the Savoy Cinema on Newry's Monaghan Street.
"Jasus, there's no friggin' heat is there?" moaned Jumpy.
"Ah, Jumpy, have ya got a hole in your wee vest, have ya?" said Po grinning.
"No, but I know where there is a big hole, and it'll be feelin' my boot!"
"Yous two are like wee girls!" snapped Red.
"It's him, that wee rat! Ya can't open your mouth and he comes out with his smart remarks!"
"Ach Jumpy, don't be like that, sure aren't ya ma friend…ma mate? Ok, so you're a pain in the arse, but sure we can't all be perfect!"
"De ya hear that, de ya? Didn't I tell ya."
Jumpy made a lunge for Po who hit him with the rolled up newspaper he was carrying. Red pulled them apart roughly.
"Will yous two act your age, will ya? I'm sick listenin' ta the pair of ya!"
Po made a face at Jumpy who replied with two fingers.

"Friggin' children, that's what I'm hangin' around with! I need ma friggin' head examined!" complained Red. "How much have ya Po?" asked Red.
"Five bob."
"Where did ya get all the money?"
"Ya remember I did some work for Johnny Marron during the week, well he paid me yesterday and I got me pocket money as well. How much have you?"
"Well, I have three bob, but I'm makin' sure two bob stays in ma pocket for the Parochial Hall tonight."
"It's the 'College Boys' tonight isn't it?" asked Jumpy.
"Yeah, I like them. I think they are one of the top three Showbands in Ireland."
"Who's your other two?" asked Po.
"The Royal and the Miami."
"I like the Miami, but I would put in the Clipper Charlton before the Royal, what about you Jumpy?"
"Well the ones ya mentioned are definitely top Showbands, but sure you're forgetting the best band ever ta come outta Northern Ireland!"
"Who's that?"
"The Freshmen."
"Jasus, I forgot about them," said Red.

Eventually they reached their destination, the rear of Hollywood's Garage at the end of Monaghan Street. Every Sunday morning there was a big game of 'Pitch and Toss' held there after ten o'clock mass. There were three big games in Newry every Sunday, one at Hollywood's, another in Dromalane and the third in Linenhall Square, otherwise known as 'The Barracks'.

The game itself was quite simple to play. Two halfpennies were placed on an 'ice lollypop' stick. Everyone would be standing in a circle around what was known as the 'Toss Area'. To gamble, you would shout out both the amount you were betting and what on. For example 'Who'll take two bob on Heads?' The Tosser himself or someone else in the circle would cover your bet. When all bets were covered, the game began. The two halfpennies were tossed into the air and allowed to land on the ground. When they settled, and a Harp and a Head were showing, they were tossed again until a pair was achieved. If you bet on, say Heads, and they came up, you would take your money back and the money that covered it.

There was a good crowd already there when they arrived. After a few hellos to some of the guys they knew, they were soon involved in the game. About an hour later Red was standing against the garage wall talking to Jimmy Cosgrave, the manager of a local football team in the 'Summer League'.
"How'd ya make out Red?"
"Couldn't win on a friggin' one horse race…you?"
"Down a few bob I think."
Po arrived jingling his bulging pocket.
"How'd ya do?" asked Red.
"Not too bad."
"Jasus, by the sound of that, a lot more than not too bad!"
"Are we headin'?"
"Yeah, where's Jones?"
"He's staying on for a while."
"Ok, let's go then, bye Jimmy," said Red.
"Bye Jimmy," added Po.
"Take care lads."

The boys had turned onto Monaghan Street before Po spoke.
"How much did ya lose?"
"I didn't."
"Ya didn't?"
"No."
"I don't understand, ya said back there ya lost."
"I know, but that was for Jimmy's benefit."
"You've lost me."
"It was his son Billy that was betting against me ya see. I took him for over three pounds!"
"Jasus, ya did well, I took almost thirty bob meself."
"Where we goin'?"
"I want to see Falsoni."

"Why ya want ta see Anto?"
"I owe him five bob and I want to pay him while I have it."

Ten minutes later the two boys were sipping coffee in Uncle Luigi's. Anto had joined them, he was working until six behind the counter.
"So what's the craic?" Anto asked putting a fourth spoonful of sugar in his coffee.
"Damn all…you?"
"So yis all made a fortune at the toss?"
"We did ok I suppose, at least we have learned when ta get out," said Po.
"That's where it's at ya know Po, gettin' out at the right time. I used to be winnin' big and then start losin' then a would double ma bets ta try an get it back, but it never worked. Who was the big winner this mornin'?"
"Your man, what's his name Red, from the Meadow…?"
"Peter Gorman, that frigger never loses."
"He never does, does he," agreed Po.
"Is there no way ta fix the toss?" asked Anto.
"Wish there was," answered Red smiling ruefully.
"There's bound ta be a way ya know," said Po thoughtfully.
Red and Anto looked at each other.
"He's off again," smiled Anto.
"Jasus Po, it's impossible. It's all down ta luck, unless ya can get a two headed coin."
"I know all that, but sometimes luck needs a little help. I'll have ta think about it."
"Well if ya do come up with somethin', let me know. I'd love ta get my money back from that guy Gorman. He took me for nearly twenty pounds a few weeks ago at poker, ya remember that Red? I was sure he and a couple of his mates were cheatin', but I couldn't prove it."
"Don't worry Anto, if there's a way, himself will find it for sure," laughed Red nodding towards Po.

Two days later Red was walking along Castle Street when he heard his name being called. Turning around he saw Po approaching at speed.
"I've done it, I've done it," he panted.

"Who did ya do it to?"
"Very funny…I know how ta fix the tossin' coins, well…almost. There's a few things I haven't figured out yet."
"Go on."
"Well, it was something we were doin' in school put it in ma head… lead."
"Lead?"
"Lead."
"Ya want ta make lead coins?"
"Don't be a moron, no, a lead coating."
"Wait a minute, ya want ta paint the coins with lead?"
"Sort of."
"I knew your one last brain cell would pack in under the strain one of these days."
"Let me explain it ta ya, thick dick."
"Go on then."
"Did ya ever drop a piece of buttered bread?"
"Yeah."
"Well, if ya think about it, nine times outta ten it will land with the buttered side down…right?"
"Suppose so…"
"I mix a tiny bit of lead with enamel copper paint and put it on a halfpenny. I did this a few times already, let it dry and tried. Every single time I tossed the coin, the lead side was down."
"But sure it would be noticed."
"No it won't. I only use a tiny wee bit, but just ta be sure it would need ta be done in a dim light."
"Ok, let's go and talk ta Anto."

****

"Hi Pete," said Po to Peter Gorman who was sitting reading the Beano in the school playground.
"Po."
"How's things?" said Po sitting down.
"Ok."
"Ya going ta Anto's tonight?"

"Anto's…what for?"
"The big toss."
"What big toss?" said Peter, his interest rising.
"Ya haven't been invited then?"
"No…what's it all about then?"
"Anto's havin' a private 'pitch and toss' out the back of the café tonight, Uncle Luigi's away for a few days, big money, invites only."
"Jasus, I never heard a thing about it. Can ya get me in?"
"If Anto didn't invite ya, how could I get ya in?"
"The bastard's afraid I'll take his money, ya gotta get me in Po."
"No can do. There's no way," said Po getting up.
Peter stood up also.
"Look, ya find a way ta get me in and ah'll give ya five bob."
"Five bob, Jasus Peter, ya must want in bad?"
"Will ya do it?"
"Well, a could do with the money…ok, I'll do ma best, but no guarantees, be in Uncle Luigi's at nine tonight."

****

Po, Anto and Red were sitting in the first snug.
"There ya go Po," said Anto sliding a pound note across the table.
"Jasus Anto, thanks."
"Without you, we couldn't a taken that bastard Gorman."
"Too true, well done wee man," added Red.
"It's been a good day all round. Ya know he gave me five bob ta get him in, you gave me a pound, and I won five quid at the toss."
"How did you do Red?" asked Anto.
"I reckon I made about eight quid, never mind us, how did you do?"
"I made my money back and maybe another twenty pound."
"Wow."
"Hi, what was all that about…givin' Gorman a free fish?"
Anto put his head down on the table and began laughing.
"I put a double dose of Uncle Luigi's jollop inside the fish. Gorman will have the scoot for a week."

The following day at school Spud Murphy came up to Red and Po at break.
"I lost a friggin' fortune last night."
"Sorry ta hear that Spud, where's Pete, I didn't see him taday?"
"I called for him this mornin'. His mom said he was up all night with diarrhoea."
"Jasus, sorry ta hear that. No laugh the scoot," said Po as he and Red turned to leave.

Po stopped and looked back at Spud.
"Ya know, it could be lead poisonin'. I heard there's a lot of it about."

End

The Blind Date

1960

"Look Po, it's your birthday tomorrow. We thought it would be a great birthday present for ya, didn't we Anto?" said Red seriously.
"He's tellin' nothin' but the truth Po."
"Him, tellin' the truth? Now there's a joke."
"Look Po, she's crazy about ya," pointed out Anto.
"He's right, that's a fact, she is," added Red.
"I wish I could place her, I can't remember her face a'tall," said Po.
"Never worry bout that Po, ya have a date with a fine bit of stuff on Thursday night," smiled Anto.
"I hear what ya'r sayin', but I'm not sure...ya know...I hate blind dates."
"Well, wantin' ta go out with you, maybe she is blind come ta think of it," laughed Red.
"Ah, sure aren't ya the funny one," sneered Po at Red.
"Look Po, look at it like this, ya have a date with a woman, who, I can tell ya is well put together. She has yokes out ta here," said Anto demonstrating with his hands.
"He's right Po, and I happen ta know ya like women with big yokes," smiled Red.

"This is all fine I know…the problem is…I just don't trust you two bastards!"
"Jasus, isn't that lovely," said Red looking at Anto.
"Well, he's your best friend after all," said Anto shaking his head.
"I know, it's hurtful when a friend doesn't trust ya isn't it?"
"Hurtful? I would be devastated so a would."
"Yeah, you're right, I am devastated Anto, hurt as well," said Red placing both hands on his heart and trying his best to look sad.
"Would ya ever piss off ya whores, yous are up ta somethin', I can feel it in me water so a can."
Red and Anto looked at each other straight faced.
"See what a mean…hurtful, untrustin', just downright unfeelin'."
"Too right…I'm just feelin' so let down, so sad, a just can't find the words…"
"Look, will you two catch yourselves on will ya?"
"Well, are ya goin' to go out with the gorgeous Lilly Meehan then?" asked Anto.
"I'm not sure."
"I'm not sure," mocked Anto.
"Anto, I was just thinkin', would she go out with me?" asked Red.
"Jasus, never thought of that, she likes ya…I know that. De ya want me to find out?"
"Yeah, why not, himself doesn't want her and she is a well built young lady ya know."
"I didn't say I wasn't goin' ta go out with her, I said was just thinkin' about it so I was," put in Po quickly.
"For Jasus sake will ya make up your mind Po. I have to tell her mate Mary tonight," Anto complained.
"Oh all right then, I'll go out with her…just ta keep yous two quiet."
"Ya know, tryin' ta get him ta agree ta anythin' is a day's work," said Anto to Red.
"You're talkin' nothin' but the truth Anto," answered Red straight faced.

****

Thursday night arrived and Red, Po and Anto were sitting in the first snug in Uncle Luigi's.
"Is your wee self all nervous Po?" smiled Red.
"No...why should I be nervous?"
"Well, first date, tryin' ta make a good impression an all that."
"And look at him...dressed up like the dog's dinner too...smellin' like a whore's handbag," added Anto. "I'll have ya know that this aftershave is expensive so it is," complained Po.
"Ya didn't fall for that one did ya Po? They told ya it was aftershave?" smiled Red.
"Don't you start Morgan...the stuff you buy would choke an elephant at forty yards."
"Po, did no one ever tell ya, aftershave? It's for people who actually shave," smiled Red.
"I shave so a do," snapped Po.
"Po, listen ta me now, shaving a dozen hairs on your face is not actually shavin'," smirked Red.
"Go suck a lemon you," Po said angrily.
Anto looked at his watch.
"It's time ya were hittin' the trail Po. It's twenty past seven already."
"You're right, ok, I'll see yis here later," said Po leaving.
"Hey Po, remember you're an altar boy now, keep your wee thing in your trousers," smiled Red.
"Ya'r so funny Morgan, ya should be on the stage, first one outta town," quipped Po as he left.
"Well?" asked Anto.
"Well what?" returned Red.
"What de ya think? Will he freak out?"
"Naw...well on the other hand, she is a wee bit big."
"Big? She weighs about twenty stone."
"True, truc," Red giggled. "Yeah...he'll freak all right."
"She'll smother him," laughed Anto.
"Well it was all your idea in the first place," said Red pointing his finger at Anto.
"Well, I owed her mate Mary a favour. When she asked me to get big Lilly a date with Po, sure a had ta do it."

"But why Po?"
"Ah…well, God love poor Lilly, she fancies the wee rat, plus, I owed that wee frigger too, but not a favour," laughed Anto.

Later that night, when the café was closed, Red and Anto met up again.
"So, any word from the big date front?" asked Anto.
"Not a peep. Haven't seen hide nor hair of him."
"Jasus…and it's twelve thirty already," said Anto looking at his watch.

Next day Red decided just after lunch to call to Po's house as he had not heard from him since the previous evening, his curiosity was getting the better of him.
Po's front door was opened by his younger brother.
"He's in his room," he shouted and disappeared.
Red made his way up the stairs to Po's room and went in. He was still in bed, but awake.
"What's up with ya then?" asked Red as he bounced down on the bed.
Po groaned in agony. "Be careful for frig sake will ya?"
"What's wrong?"
"Nothin'."
"Come on Hillen…what's wrong…tell me?"
"No."
"Tell me?" Red raised his voice.
"Ya wouldn't believe me anyway."
"Of course I would, what happened?"
Po made a painful effort to sit up.
"If I tell ya…ya promise not ta say a word ta anyone, especially that bastard Anto?"
"Ok…so…?"
"Well, I met your one last night. Ya didn't tell me she drank?"
"I didn't know."
"And ya didn't tell me ya bastard that she was the size of a mountain either."
Red was finding it very difficult to keep his face straight.
"Well, she's not all that big…just a wee bit overweight maybe."

"A wee bit overweight…are ya out a your friggin' mind…she's the size of a tank."
"Well…so what?"
"I met her and we went for a walk out Ashgrove."
"And…?"
"She had a bottle of whiskey in her bag and kept swiggin' from it."
"Did ya get a drink at least?" smiled Red.
"Funny…yeah, I got a drink…needed one for sure."
"And…?"
"Well…after a while she got a bit…ya know?"
"What?"
"Ya know? Randy."
"I knew she had problems that girl."
"Will ya shut up…do ya want ta hear or not?"
"Sorry, go on…go on."
"Well, she started kissin' me…ya know…and I sorta lost ma balance."
"Lost your balance?"
"Yeah…lost ma friggin' balance ok…a fell backwards."
Red laughed.
"Ya fell down on the job…ya auld ejit."
"That wasn't the worst of it…"
"It wasn't…?"
Po groaned as he changed position.
"Didn't she only fall on top of me!"
She…fell…on top…of ya?"
Red lost control. He just could not hold it back any longer. He slid down to the floor with his face in his hands and roared.
"Yeah…go on and have a good laugh ya bastard."
"And…what…happened?" Red managed to get out.
There was no answer from Po. Red got up and sat down gently on the side of the bed again.
"Tell me…what happened then?"
Po mumbled something Red didn't hear.
"What?"
"I broke three whorin' ribs so a did."

This was just too much for Red. He just could not handle it. He almost fell down himself he laughed so hard. Some five minutes later Red had settled down and was able to talk again…in a sort of sobbing voice.
"And…you broke…ribs…then?"
"I spent the friggin' night in the friggin' hospital so I did."
"In the hospital…huh?"
"Now you promised ya wouldn't tell anybody," said Po pointing at Red.
"I did…I did."
"Not a word…ya promised."
"Not a word…I swear."
"Some friggin' birthday present that was. See the next time I have a birthday, I'm not tellin' ya when it is."
Red left Po promising to call back later that night. He went straight to Uncle Luigi's, found Anto, and dragged him by the sleeve out the back and sat him down on some bags of potatoes.
"Now…get ready…I'm not supposed ta tell ya this…but…"

End

Valentine's Day

1960

"Now, ya give me your word of honour ya won't forget?" said Po to Red.
"Look, I said I'd post the stupid thing, didn't I?"
"It's very important. I promised her I'd send her one," went on Po.
"I thought these Valentine's things were supposed ta be anonymous?"
"The rest of the ones I sent out yesterday were, but this one's special."
"Ah Jasus, you're in love with wee Patricia are ya?"
"Piss off ya bastard, Morgan."
"An if ya don't get a card from her, sure ya'll just die."
"You're just jealous, so ya are."
"Jealous, are ya outta your mind, are ya? Sure, that wee girl wouldn't be interested in me. She has a thing for small wee men who have small wee willies and pimples on their bums."
"Who told ya I had pimples on ma bum?"
"Your ma did."
"Jasus."
"Why, was it a big secret or somethin'?"
"Well, ya wouldn't want your bum to be the topic of conversation now, would ya?"

"Well, I have it from good sources that your bum has been the topic of conversation and in the dreams too, of a few nice boys, over in Edward Street."
"Who said that?" snapped Po angrily.
"Can't say, sworn to total and absolute secrecy by the Newry Fruits and Queers Association."
"Jasus, you're a friggin', whorin' bastard, Morgan."
"Thanks," laughed Red.
"Seriously," said Po as he parted from Red. "Now don't forget ta post the card."
"Right, right."

Later, Red did, in fact, post the card to Patricia, a girl Po had being dating for a few weeks. He smiled as he popped it into the post box. He called into Uncle Luigi's, on his way home to see Anto, who was working in the cafe. He sat in the first snug and ordered some coffee from Bridget, the waitress. A few moments later, Anto sat down beside him, drying his hands with a towel.
"Well, what's happenin'?" he asked.
Red related his conversation with Po earlier, and how he was panicking about the card he was sending to Patricia.
"A wonder did he send one ta your woman, Lilly?"
"Lilly?"
"Jasus Christ, don't tell me ya forgot about your big one that he went out with, that fell on him and nearly crushed him ta death?"
"De ya know a had forgot about her," laughed Red.
"Well she hasn't forgotten about Po. She was in here the other night, and tortured me with questions about him."
"Are ya serious? She has a thing for Po?"
"She's friggin' nuts about him," smiled Anto.
"Well what about that?" said Red, rubbing his chin.
"What are ya plannin'?"
"Well a was just thinkin'. Wouldn't it just make her day if she were ta get a really nice Valentine's card from Po?"
"Ah Jasus, sure that's only brilliant," smiled Anto, slapping his hand on the table.
"Will ya get one, Anto, sometime taday?"

"Leave it with me. Come in tonight at closin' and we'll fill it out together."
"Done."

Later that night, Red arrived at Uncle Luigi's, just at closing time. After helping with the cleaning up, both Anto and himself, sat at a table on their own, and began filling in Po's Valentine's card to Lilly.
"Now, make it look like he's really crazy about her, Anto."
"Let's see… 'Roses are red, violets are blue, my willie was made, just for you'."
"Excellent!" roared Red.
"How about, 'When I met you first I knew right then. That I was your cock and you were my hen'."
"Brilliant, where did ya learn all these things?" laughed Red.
Anto produced a little handbook from his back pocket and laid it on the table, in front of Red.
Lifting it, Red read out the title, "The Thinking Man's Valentine's Guide."
"Ya can't be leavin' important things like this ta chance now, can ya?" laughed Anto.
"Jasus, ya'r like a wee scout, sure ya are. Always be prepared."
"My motto. Now we'll get this finished, go and post it, so it will go in the first post in the mornin'."
"Sounds good ta me," smiled Red, as they both got their heads down to finishing Po's Valentine's surprise.

Two days later, the big day arrived, and Po was standing outside Red's door, waiting for him at eight fifteen, in the morning. Red came out, bleary eyed, and closed the door behind him.
"What are ya doin' here, Hillen? I always call for ya when I'm passin', don't I?"
"Couldn't wait ta show ya, here, hold my schoolbag."
Po fumbled in his pocket, and produced a number of cards.
"They came in the early post. Now de ya see this one. I'm nearly sure that's from Phyllis McParland."
"The wee skinny one, with the big yokes?"
"That's her."

"Why would she be sendin' ya a card?"
"I think she secretly fancies me."
"Oh God, I really need this, first thing in the mornin'."
"Now this one's from Patricia, she signed it. Smell it, she put her perfume on it, too."
"Take that thing away from ma face, it stinks."
"I can't figure out the third one, yet. It could be one of two I have in mind."
"Wonderful, now shut up, ya've given me a headache."
"How many cards did ya get?"
"I don't know, I didn't look at the post."
"Jasus, you're a cool one. I was waitin' on the postman, so a was."
"I'll have one from Maureen, for sure. That'll be the only one."
"Ah, ya poor wee unloved person," comforted Po, patting Red's back.
"Would ya ever go and…"
"Now Red, no bad talk on lovers' day. Ya have ta be nice ta everyone."
"That just applies ta humans. I can say what a want ta you."
"Oh, very funny, hilarious."

Later, that day, Red and Po walked into Uncle Luigi's. Anto wasn't there, but Jammy greeted them.
"Ah sure, ya just missed your one, what's her face. She was lookin' for ya Po."
"Who?"
"Her, the big one you were out with."
"Lilly?"
"Aye, that's her."
"Shit."
"Your wee self is in demand, Po."
"Frig off, she's the last one I want ta see."
"I thought ya had a big thing with her," whispered Red.
"Yeah, I did have a big thing, with her. She nearly killed me."
"Well, looks like she's back for more. Frig me Po, ya must've impressed her, ya romantic wee devil."
"Piss off, you."
Just then, Anto walked into the café.

"Ah, you're here, then. I was just talkin' to your one, Lilly. She was lookin' for ya, she's on her way here, now. Well Red, what's the craic?"
"Nothin', you?"
"A have ta tell ya about the card I got this mornin'. Are yis sittin' down."
"Yeah, where did Po go?"
"Don't know…Hi Bridget, where did Po go?" Anto asked the waitress.
"He just went past me like a sprinter, and out the back of the shop. Looked like he saw a ghost," she smiled.
"Hello Anto, Red."
They both looked around to see the large frame of Po's one time blind date, Lilly, standing at the table.
"Hello Lilly, are ya sittin' down for a while?" asked Anto.
"Just for a minute, have ta meet ma sister."
"Ya know this is a coincidence, Po was here a little while ago and was talkin' about ya."
"Was he, really? What did he say?"
"Well, sure he only has a big crush on ya. Sure, ya know that anyway," smiled Red.
"Oh my God, has he really?"
"Gives me a pain in the head the way he keeps goin' on about ya," added Anto.
"Ahhh, isn't he a wee doll?"
"Well, I wouldn't go that far, Lilly," smiled Red.
"When will he be in again?"
"He will be here tonight, sometime," said Anto.
"I'll call in about ten, then," said Lilly, standing up.
"I'll tell him. Once he knows you'll be here, sure there's nothin' on earth will keep him out," said Red, seriously.
"Ahhh, tell him I'm lookin' forward ta seein' him."
"Don't worry, we will," assured Anto.
After Lilly waved goodbye at the door, Anto was the first to speak.
"I don't care if ya have to tie him up and drag him here. You make sure he's here tonight, at ten. I wouldn't miss this for anythin'."
"Oh don't ya worry, I'll have the wee bugger here. Its pay back time for all the tricks that wee frigger has played on me."

****

"I don't know what all the fuss is about, anyway. Why does he want us there?"
"Po, look, ya know Anto as well as I do. He wants ta show off the cards he got. Sure, he's our mate, we have ta go along ta keep him happy."
"Suppose."
The two walked into Uncle Luigi's at exactly five minutes to ten. A broadly smiling Anto was behind the counter, working.
"Well Red, Po, ya havin' a coffee?"
"Yeah, love one," said Red, winking at Anto.
"Me too."
Red elbowed Po. "Did ya get any cards Anto?"
"Loads, wait till ya see them."
They sat down in the first snug. A few moments later, Anto arrived with the coffee. He looked to the side and smiled, then back at Po. Here's someone comin' ta see ya, I think, Po."
Po leaned out of the snug and pulled back, quickly.
"Oh holy Jasus."
"What is it?" asked Red, innocently.
"It's only friggin' Lilly," whispered Po.
"Well, I'm off, out the back, ta do some work," smiled Anto.
"Ah, isn't that nice, sure she'll be glad ta see ya, I'll leave yous ta have a wee love chat. I'll go out back, and talk ta Anto."
"Ya'll stay where ya are, ya bastard," snarled Po.
"Hi Anto, hi Red, and Po. It's really nice to see ya," said Lilly, as she slid into the snug beside Po. She had to squeeze hard to fit between the table and the seat, but she made it. There was no way out, now, for Po. He was trapped.
"Come on, Red, we'll leave the young lovers to talk their sweet talk," smiled Anto.
"Naw, yous are ok, stay here," said Po, making all sorts of threatening faces at Red.
"Anto, come on, sure we'll leave these young lovers ta hold hands and stuff. We don't want ta be gooseberries, do we Anto?"
"For sure."
"Morgan, a hope your ma never finds your real da."

"Bye for now, wee Po," Red put his arm around Anto as he stood up. "Doesn't it make ya feel all mushy inside ta see young lovers?"
"Mushy, pure mushy," grinned Anto, as they walked away, leaving their mate to a fate worse than death.
"Hey, bastards," they both turned back to look at Po.
"I have a long memory, yous rotten whores."
They both smiled, looked at each other, and looked back at Po and Lilly.
"Would ya look at that, Red. A match made in heaven," smiled Anto, tilting his head to one side.
"Made for each other, for sure. It was the angels that brought them together, ya know," added Red.
"Ya know you're right, it was two angels that brought them together," said Anto.
"Aren't they just lovely?" said Lilly, cuddling up to Po.
"Friggin' beautiful," snarled a white-faced Po.

Fifteen minutes later, Po and Lilly were walking along Hill Street. Lilly had talked him into walking her home.
"Isn't it great we have some time to ourselves alone Po?" smiled Lilly.
"Brilliant."
"We can head over Monaghan Street. That's the long way home, but at least that way we can have more time ta talk," giggled Lilly.

Po looked up when he heard a loud laugh and shouting in front of them. He immediately recognized Dapper Ruddy and a couple of his mates. Dapper was a well known local bully and so-called 'hard man'.
"Let's cross the road here," said Po quickly.
"Why here?" asked Lilly.
"Those guys up ahead are nothin' but trouble. A don't want anythin' ta do with them," answered Po looking down.
Before Lilly could answer the loud voice of Dapper Ruddy made them both look up.
"Well, well. If it isn't Mighty Mouse and with Wee Lilly, as well. Wow, isn't that a sight for sore eyes?"
His friends laughed loudly on cue. They blocked the footpath, stopping Po and Lilly.

"Goin' somewhere nice, are we?" smirked Dapper.
"Bit late for you ta be out, Dapper. There's no kids out at this time of night for ya ta push around," challenged Po.
Dapper's face turned into an angry snarl. He lunged forward and pushed Po with both hands, almost knocking him down. Lilly stepped forward putting herself between Po and Dapper. "Ok Dapper, that's enough. Leave him alone."
Dapper reached out and slowly ran the back of his hand down Lilly's face.
"So do ya want ta play with me Lilly? It'll be more fun than with the wee runt there."
She brushed his hand aside with annoyance. Dapper's friends giggled loudly. Po tried to lunge forward again at Dapper only to be stopped by Lilly's outstretched arm. She moved a little closer to Dapper looking right into his eyes.
"Dapper, ya'r so nice. A always wanted ta play with ya."
A moment later, before Dapper could answer, Lilly landed the most perfect right hook you ever saw on Dapper's jaw. He was unconscious before he hit the ground. His two mates looked at each other and then at Lilly.
"Yes? Any of you want to try your luck?" snarled Lilly.
Dapper's two mates swapped glances again and took off at speed along Hill Street.
Po stepped forward and looked down at Dapper.
"Jasus Lilly, you're somethin' else. What'll we do about him?"
"Nothin'. Just leave him there. If he doesn't wake till mornin' the dustmen will lift him. Come on, let's go home."

The next day Red and Anto were sitting in the first snug in Uncle Luigi's, drinking coffee, when Po arrived. He slid into the snug, smiling.
"Well, if it isn't love's lost dream," smiled Anto.
"Good morning bastards," replied Po.
"Ah no, Lilly must have been too much for the wee man. Ya can see he is lookin' confused and groggy," said Red with a look of false concern on his face.
"Ya could be right, Red. He does look a bit odd. Well, he always looks a bit odd, but a bit odder this mornin'," put in Anto.

Red reached across the table and felt Po's forehead with the back of his hand.

"Well, a don't think he has a temperature."

Po sat, smiling with his arms crossed, nodding.

"Can ya speak, Po? Just make a sign."

Po made a sign at Red with his index finger.

"So what's the craic, anything excitin' happenin'?" asked Po.

Red and Anto exchanged glances. They both reached across and began hugging Po who promptly pushed them away.

"Frig off, ya fairies."

"Ok now, Po. Leave nothin' out, right? We want ta hear every detail," demanded Red.

"Start at the beginnin' and tell all, Po. Leave nothin' out," added Anto.

"Well, there's not a lot ta tell yis, lads," said Po leaning back and looking up at the ceiling. "A left Lilly home. We chatted for a while, and a kissed her goodnight."

"Ya'r lying through ya'r teeth. What really happened?" prompted Anto.

"Well, that's all that happened. Well, maybe the fact that Lilly decked Dapper Ruddy. But other than that, nothing really happened a'tall."

Anto almost fell off the bench to get closer to Po.

"What?"

"It's just as a told ya. Nothin' happened."

Red reached across and grabbed Po's coat.

"Let me kill him."

Anto pulled Red off Po.

"Now Red, settle down. We want ta hear what happened first. Ya can kill him later. Now Po, tell your good friends, Red and me, what happened with Dapper Ruddy."

Po related the story to his two mates in detail who both sat open-mouthed throughout.

"Jasus!" was the response at the end of the story from both of them in unison.

"And Jasus, again," added Anto.

"Well, that's how it happened. If a had not been there, a wouldn't have believed it, me own self," said Po, sipping Red's coffee.

"If a was asked ta come up with somethin' to happen ta that bastard Ruddy, a could not have come up with a better one than this. Knocked out by a girl. Frig me, he'll never hold his head up, again," laughed Red. "The boys at school will destroy him. Can ya just imagine? 'Hi, Ruddy, behave yourself or I'll get ma sister for ya'."
"It's just perfect. The downfall of a bully," laughed Anto.
"Well, de ya see? We did ya a favour Po, gettin' ya all fixed up with Lilly," smiled Red.
"More of a favour than ya know, lads. Ya see, a now have a bodyguard. She has a right hook that would take Joe Lewis out. So all my days of being tortured by you whores is over. Any more messin' from you lot an' a will just tell Lilly yis are givin' me a hard time. Then, a sure would not like ta be in your shoes."
Red and Anto exchanged glances.
"Red, go and get me a Coke. Anto, get me a chip, an be quick about it."
Red and Anto swapped glances and both grabbed Po at the same time, slapping his head, and pushing cold chips into his face. There was some colourful language added.
"I'm warnin' yis, I'll tell Lilly on yis and ya'll be for it," shouted Po from behind his arms.

Valentine's Day. A day for lovers, a day when they come into each other arms, albeit, sometimes, reluctantly!

The New Cart

1960

As Red approached the group no one paid any attention. A hive of industry enveloped them all, each having their jobs, some practical and some advisory. Red's Uncle Pajoe and Po were fitting the wheels to the new cart. Anto and Jumpy were putting the final touches to the bodywork and Topcoat was watching closely and occasionally adding advice or criticism which was usually answered with a grunt or swear word.

"Well, how's it goin'?" Red asked Pajoe.
"Goin' well, the wheels turned out better than we hoped. They fitted the new stronger axles perfectly."
"Friggin' perfectly," added Po. "This will be a flyer for sure."
"She'll be the fastest thing in the town and that's no lie," stated Anto with commitment.
"I still think she would have got more speed if that back axle had been moved forward more, allowing the weight to be more in the middle," said Topcoat with hand on chin.
"How do ya mean, the weight….?" Red began to ask.
"No," they all seemed to shout in unison. "Don't ask him!"

"What?" laughed Red.

"He," said Po pointing at Topcoat, "Mr. Foreman, pain in the arse Topcoat, has done frig all but complain about every single thing we did all day."

"I was only tryin' to keep ya right," complained Topcoat, hands outstretched.

It took around two minutes for all the obscenities to be said and all the loose bits of material lying around to be thrown at Topcoat.

"So when will she be ready for a try out?" Red asked Pajoe.

"She's ready right now. We just have to attach the body and she's a go."

"Right, I think we'll try her out on Hyde Market, what de ya think?"

"I'm taking her, remember that," said Po forcefully pointing his finger at Red.

"Am I arguin'?"

"Just in case ya do."

"Now Po…"

"Don't you start givin' me your 'now Po' voice Morgan."

Red looked at Jumpy and Anto.

"Did ya ever see the likes of it? He's worse than a wee girl fightin' over a doll."

"Ach Red, now don't be pickin' on our wee hard worker and skilful cart driver," smiled Anto.

"Right…right, I'm awful sorry Po. Now don't get your wee knickers in a twist. She's all yours just like we promised."

"If I hadn't got the wheels there'd be no cart a'tall," Po pointed out.

"…and don't forget I'm chief mechanic," added Jumpy.

"Right Jumpy, you're chief mechanic, we won't forget," said Anto winking at Red.

"Now, you've all forgotten a very important thing here ya know," said Pajoe looking up at the gang.

"What's that?" asked Red.

"Yous haven't given her a name yet."

"Jasus…never thought of that," mused Anto.

"Sure it's obvious," put in Topcoat. "Since she will be the fastest cart in the town, ya should call her…'The Bullet'."

"Hi, that's not bad a'tall," agreed Po.

"No…can't…Joey Grimes calls his cart 'Bullet'."
"Shit," put in Topcoat. "But wait a minute, sure we will just add somethin' to it then."
"What de ya mean?" asked Jumpy.
"Well…let's see…she was built here in Castle Street, so how about…'The Castle Street Bullet'?"
"That's perfect, that's the name," beamed Po.
"Are we all agreed then?" asked Red.
Nods and smiles all round affirmed the new cart was now officially christened.

****

"Now keep her straight!" said Anto seriously.
"And make sure ya stay in the middle of the road," commented Jumpy.
"Brake nice and early Po…don't leave it to the last minute."
"Watch that hole in the road outside McCoy's Po, Naffy McKay lost a wheel there yesterday."
"Jasus will ya all piss off…I know what I'm doin'. Ya'd think I never took a cart down here before ta hear you lot."
"Frig me, sorry I opened ma mouth ya wee shit," complained Anto stepping back.
"Now Anto be kind to the child, he's nervous ya know," smiled Red.
"I'm not friggin' nervous ya dick. Now, will yous get back and let me go?"
"Ok now…hang on," said Red who had moved to the back of the cart and was massaging Po's shoulders.
"Right…ok…one…two…three …go."
Red released Po and The Castle Street Bullet with the help of gravity, began its maiden run on the steep Hyde Market hill. A cheer came from all there, as Po gathered speed quickly heading towards the bottom of the hill in the direction of Hill Street.
The cart was indeed fast and handled well. As Po reached the halfway point he began to apply the brake which was a one inch square piece of wood bolted to the side of the cart with another length travelling underneath. Both pieces of wood had pieces of thin metal wrapped

around the ends covering about three inches. When Po pulled back the handle, the metal ends pushed against the two back solid rubber tyres therefore slowing down the cart. At the bottom of the hill Po steered to the left to avoid hitting the footpath and brought the Castle Street Bullet to a sliding halt. Almost immediately he was having his back slapped, hair tossed, punches on the arms and a chorus of…'Well done and friggin' brilliant'.
"Well, she's the fastest thing I've ever rode, I can tell ya that," panted Po standing up.
"She went like the wind," put in Jumpy excitedly.
"Ya were down the hill like Sterling Moss for sure," commented a smiling Anto.
"Right, now let's get her home and remember, tell no one about her, other than we have a new cart, right?" said Red loudly, pointing his finger at everyone there.
All agreed.

****

There were ten carts entered in the Great Cart Race the following Sunday. The race was held on the first Sunday of every month and a cash prize, which would be the total entrance fees of two shillings and sixpence (half crown) per cart, went to the winner. However, a lot more money would be made on the side betting which of course was organised by Anto. There were five heats on this Sunday, Po and the Castle Street Bullet was in the first.

"Now Po, win, but only just, ok?" whispered Red.
"Don't worry, a understand. I'll hold her back and make it look good."
Shifty was the starter and had a chequered flag, made from an old apron, of which he was very proud. For races, a wooden wedge was placed in front of the cart's back wheel. A piece of string was attached to the wedge and on the starters command the wedges would be pulled away and the carts would begin the downhill run. This was felt to be the fairest way to start ensuring that no cart would have an advantage over any other. Shifty, checked that both carts were ready. Po's opponent in

this heat was Whitey Hanna, who had a pretty good cart himself and had won the race on a number of occasions.

Shifty stood in the middle of the road, a few yards in front of the carts. He began the count down making sure that the two other officials were ready to pull the chucks away.
"Ready…one…two…three…go!"
Both chucks were pulled away and the carts began to move downhill gathering speed as they went. For almost two thirds of the race they were both nose to nose then Po moved almost effortlessly in front and went on to win the race by half a length. Po had an almost repeat performance in the second race and was now in the final. He was sitting on the steps at the top of Hyde Market while the chief mechanic Jumpy was checking out every nut and bolt on the cart.
"I'll just do the same as a have been doing…huh?" said Po to Red.
"No way, absolutely not. Now, ya don't hold her back…let her go from the start. This guy Thompson has a good cart. I've been watchin' him in the last race and that cart is fast I can tell ya."
"Ok…I'll let her go, but sure it'll be a cake walk," smiled Po.
"Well Anto is hopin' so, there is a lot of money ridin' on the race. The holdin' back did the job for Anto he says. Thompson is the favourite and you are two ta one."
"Shit."
"Shit what?"
"We are goin' ta have ta get another bookie here sometime. We can't even have a bet cause Anto wouldn't take it."
"Well, sure ya wouldn't expect him ta would ya? Anyway, sure we still get 20% from him anyway."
"I know, but think how we would be doin' if we had a tenner on?"
"Yeah…nice."
"Castle Street Bullet," came the booming voice of Shifty who was now in his official role as starter again. There were three carts in the final, Po, Paddy Thompson and Dicker Gorman.
The starter checked they were all in line and ready. He began the start countdown.
"Carts…one…two…three…go!"
Po immediately took the lead and was increasing it.

"Jasus…he's forgot the friggin' hole at McCoys so he has," shouted Anto over the din.
Anto was right, Po did forget the hole. He hit it with his right wheel. The cart began to bounce wildly and swing to the right. Po had almost been thrown off but seemed to be hanging on…just.

They were nearing the bottom of the hill and the finish line. Po was still in the lead by a few inches at this point but Paddy Thomson had made ground on him and was catching up fast. There were just a few yards to go when Red noticed Po lean to the left and pull the right hand side of the cart up.
'What's the friggin' ejit doin now?' Red thought.
Po seemed to increase speed just then and crossed the line in first place. Red and the rest of the team raced to the bottom of the hill and found Po leaning forward getting his breath back.
"What happened?" asked Red as he arrived.
"I hit that friggin' hole didn't I?" complained Po. "I forgot there were three carts in the race, normally there are only the two. There was no way I could miss the bastardin' thing."
"What were ya doing there at the end?" continued Red.
"See that…?" Po was pointing at the right front wheel. There was a definite buckle to be seen.
"It was pullin' me all over the place so I got the bright idea of leanin' ta one side and liftin' the wheel off the road…it worked."
"Jasus," commented Jumpy.
"Ya were lucky, ya could have lost control altogether ya know."
"With my skill? Ya must be jokin'."
Before Po could duck, Red's hand caught him on the back of the head.
"Cheeky wee bastard."
Anto had now arrived.
"That was friggin' close Po, are ya tryin' ta give me a heart attack?" panted Anto.
"It was pure skill and balance…what can a tell ya?" smiled Po.
This time he was ready and got out of the way of Anto's swinging hand.

Later as they sat in Uncle Luigi's eating their free fish and chips supplied by Anto. Shifty McShane was ensuring he would not be left out of the day's historical memories.
"It's not everyone that can start a race with such style ya know," boasted Shifty. "It's all in the timin' and the arm motion."
"Jasus, will ya listen ta your man over there," said Red, nodding towards Shifty.
"Listen ta him? I have a friggin' pain in my head listenin' ta him," snarled Po.
"Well, we won and that's the main thing. Anto made money, we made a few bob and Po's head has got an inch bigger," smiled Red.
"We'll call it the golf win so we will," smiled Po looking at the ceiling.
"The what?" asked Topcoat.
"The golf win…think about it…I got the hole on the way down…and I won…so ya could say I got a 'Hole in One'."
There was a moment of silence whilst everyone there exchanged glances.
"I think it's that time Red," said Anto smiling at Red.
"Ya know, a think you're right."

Po was unceremoniously grabbed and dragged out the back of the café where his head was placed under a water tap.
"Add this Po…it's a 'Tap In'," laughed Anto.

End

The Death Run

1960

"If ya had a mind, I'd tell ya, ya were out of it," said Red looking straight at his mate Po.
"But no one has ever done it before," pleaded Po.
"So what?"
"I'll be the first. I'll go down in the history books."
"You'll go down in six feet of clay, that's where you'll go."
The two were sitting in the snug nearest the front door of Uncle Luigi's. It was a Saturday morning and Anto was working on the ice cream counter. He decided to take his break when Red and Po arrived. Sitting down beside them he noticed Red was looking a bit serious.
"What's goin' on?" he asked Red.
"That stupid wee bastard's gettin' on ma nerves," growled Red nodding towards Po.
"So…what's new? He gets on everybody's nerves," smiled Anto as he sipped his coffee.
"Ya'll not believe what he wants ta do now…he only wants ta take the new cart on the Daredevil Run."
"Wow, that would be somethin' all right," smiled Anto over his cup.

"Wow shite...he not only wants to do the run, but wants to start from the Windmill Road!"
"Yeah, of course he does," laughed Anto.
"Anto...I'm not jokin'."
Anto slowly put his cup on the table and looked at Po.
"Ya are jokin'...right?"
"Look...nobody's ever done it before Anto. It would be a first," said Po seriously.
"And a last...that's not a daredevil run, that's a death run," replied Anto.
"Red...tell me he's not serious? He can't be."
"He is serious. I've been tryin' ta talk some sense ta him this past half hour, might as well talk ta that friggin' wall."
"Jasus, ya do know ya need ta talk ta a doctor or somethin' don't ya Po?" said Anto.
"Look, there's no one that can handle the Castle Street Bullet better than me. I've looked at the run loads of times over this past week and it can be done...and I'm the one that can do it."
Anto looked at Red.
"He could be killed or worse ya know...that I can live with...but when I think of the time we put into buildin' that cart, the thoughts of it piled up against a wall in bits is just too much to think about."
"Very funny, sure you're a laugh a minute Anto. Look, if ya will listen ta me for a minute I'll explain how it can be done. If I stay to the right all the way down ta the left hand bend at the John of God's Hospital, then ease to the other side of the road, cuttin' the corner...at the bottom, all I have to do is swing right into Castle Street and the hill will slow her down."
"And there ya've hit on just one of the problems, have ya the remotest idea what speed ya will be doin' when ya try ta turn into Castle Street? She'll flip for sure," pointed out Red.
"No, I've thought a that. If I use my body weight and lean into the bend it'll stop her from flippin'...ya know what a mean?"
"Po...look, it's just simply crazy. The normal run from the St. John of God's is bad enough; as far as I know there's only a few, including yourself, that have done it. A lot more have tried and ended up in

hospital...like what's his face from Church Street...?" Anto was looking at Red now for help.
"That was your man Jonso Lennon," said Red.
"That's him...he ended up with a broken leg and a broken arm... Jasus he was lucky he didn't kill himself."
"Look, I know what ya'r sayin', I've worked it out in detail. I can do it... and Anto...think about the book on it? How many people de ya think will bet that I won't do it?"
"Red...can he do it?"
"Now don't be putting me on the friggin' spot Anto...you've changed your tune now that ya heard the word money."
"No a haven't...I still think it's crazy...but if he could do it...Jasus!"
"I give up...the two of ya are out of your tree. He'll end up on a slab...I'm tellin' ya."
"Ach Red...don't be an auld granny. I can do it...I know I can. I wouldn't chance it if I thought for a minute it couldn't be done," pleaded Po.
"I don't know..."
"Come on Red...we'll make history."
"Look...this is what we'll do. I want to see ya do the Daredevil Run first ta see how she handles...right? If...and I stress...if...she handles ok...well then, a might think about it."
They all shook hands and the tentative agreement was made.

The following afternoon Po did the Daredevil Run on the Castle Street Bullet and made it look easy. He in fact did it three times just to satisfy Red.

****

The day the gang had named the 'Death Run' had arrived. A large crowd had gathered along the route from the Windmill Road junction all the way down Courtney Hill to Abbey Yard at the bottom and even into Castle Street. Stewards had been recruited to keep the road clear. They wore white handkerchiefs tied around their upper arms. The all-clear was given and everything was ready. Shifty had borrowed a stop watch so that they could time the run.

Red and Anto were kneeling beside the cart oiling the joints. Topcoat was in his official capacity as chief Steward, ordering people back to the side of the road. Shifty was of course there with his chequered flag at the ready.
It was time to go. Red leaned down to Po.
"Now don't go friggin' mad Po…right? Take her handy."
"Right Mom," smiled Po.
"Are we all set?" Shifty asked Po. He got answered with the thumbs up.
Ok…Ready…Steady."
Po lowered his upper body and tightened his grip on the steering rope. He took a deep breath…
"Go."
Shifty did a jump in the air waving his flag and ended up on his backside.
Red pushed Po's back and the Castle Street Bullet was on its way into the history books…whatever happened.

The cart began to gather speed rapidly as the hill dipped steeply. Along the sides of the route people were cheering and waving as Po sped past. Red, Anto and the rest of the gang who were at the start were running at top speed down the hill trying to keep Po in sight. He was now almost at the halfway stage, the left hand bend at St. John of God's Hospital. The cart was travelling very fast indeed, even faster than Po had imagined. Remembering his plan he gently moved to the right side of the road and then back into the bend keeping the cart as straight as possible. Making it through the bend without incident he was now on the steepest part of the hill which passed the Abbey Primary School. On the left was the St. John of God's Hospital which housed a chapel. Po smiled to himself as he almost allowed his right hand to make the sign of the cross. The wheels of the cart were now bouncing on the road. Po began to find the steering difficult. In his mind he began to get images of losing control. He shook his head as if in defiance and concentrated on the road ahead. He could see the group of people in Abbey Yard; he was now only seconds away from the most difficult point on the run… the turn into Castle Street. Pulling the steering rope to the right he could feel the cart begin to turn, but not enough…he was under-steering.

He needed to lock the wheels more…the cart was beginning to lift to the left. Po could see the right front wheel beginning to come off the ground. He remembered his plan and immediately leaned to his right as much as he could. The wheels hit the road again with a shudder and for a split second he almost lost control but managed to straighten up as the cart began the gentle climb into Castle Street…coming to a halt outside Minnie Keenan's shop. A crowd began gathering around the cart to congratulate Po on his great feat. As he was getting up the cart lurched to one side.

Just then, a panting Red and the rest of the gang arrived on the scene. He knelt down to see what the problem was with the cart only to find that the axle had broken at the right wheel.

"Jasus Christ Po…" panted Red. "If that had happened thirty seconds ago…"

Red looked at Po. The colour of his face had changed drastically, from being flushed to a sort of grey pallor.

Thirty minutes later they were all sitting in Uncle Luigi's drinking Cokes.

"Well…ya did it," said a smiling Red with his arm around Po's shoulders.

"Yeah."

"Is that all ya have ta say…yeah?"

"Yeah."

"Jasus, I thought ya would've been over the moon…tellin' us, 'Told ya so'," mocked Red.

"Ya should've stopped me ya know…when I saw that friggin' axle it scared the shit outta me," said Po looking at Red.

"What?"

"I could a been killed so a could."

"I argued with ya for an hour ta talk ya out of it ya wee frigger and ya wouldn't listen."

"Well, if ya had been a good mate ya would have argued with me for two hours so ya would."

"Anto…do ya believe this wee shit?"

"There there Po, sure ya are the talk of the town, a hero, all the women will be mad after ya."
"Ya think so?"
"Sure…women love heroes, daredevils and that."
"Never thought a that," mused Po.
"They'll be throwin' themselves at ya," added Red.
"But, that's the last death run you're doin' I can tell ya," added Red.
"For once, I'll agree with ya," smiled Po.
"How'd the bettin' go Anto?" asked Red.
"Ah…nearly forgot…this is for our hero," smiled Anto handing Po a £5 note.
"Jasus…£5...are ya sure Anto?"
"Ya deserve it…I did well outta it, here's two for your own self Red."
"Jasus…thanks Anto."

Later Red and Po were walking up Mill Street on their way home.
"Well it's all over now," said Red almost to himself.
"It is, even though I was scared shitless, I'm glad a done it."
"Ya know you're not wise, don't ya?" smiled Red.
"I know…but it was just somethin' a had ta do."
"Rather you than me."
"We'll need a stronger axle for the front ya know?"
Red stopped and looked at Po.
"Why will we need a stronger axle for the front?" he asked seriously.
"It's just something I was thinkin' about…ya know…there is that other run…"
"What other run?"
Po just smiled and began walking again. Red grabbed his shoulder and swung him around.
"What other run?"
"Well, no one has ever done High Street," smiled Po.
"What?" roared Red.
"High Street…"
"No, no, no, no way, no how."
"But…"
"No."

Red was now walking fast toward Po who was in full retreat backwards.
"But wait till a tell ya..."
Po was now running with Red hot on his tail.
"But it's never been done before," shouted Po over his shoulder.
"And you will never be able to do it either..." shouted Red still in pursuit.
"Dead people can't steer carts..."

End

The River Monster

1960

It was lunchtime on that summer Sunday as the group was engaged in the usual heated debate outside Uncle Luigi's. The August sun was hot that day having no clouds to block its view of the beautiful Irish landscape below.

"Look Po, do ya think I'm stupid altogether, do ya?" asked Dunno.
"Yeah, but what's that got to do with anythin'?" smiled Po.
"Dunno, it's well known around Newry. There's been loads a people that have seen it," put in Red.
"Have you seen it?" Dunno asked.
"No…but I don't swim there very often," replied Red.
"Yeah…right," mumbled Dunno.
"Hang on a mo, I know who ta ask," said Po turning into Uncle Luigi's.
He arrived a few moments later with Anto in tow drying his hands with a towel.
"Ok Dunno…ask Anto."
"Ask me what?"

“Po’s tryin’ ta tell me there’s a monster in the County River,” laughed Dunno.
“So?”
“Come on Anto, don’t you try and tell me ya believe it too.”
“What’s ta believe…sure it’s a fact, everybody knows that for God’s sake.”
“Ok then, so tell me this, de ya know anyone who’s seen it then?” asked Dunno.
“Sure, didn’t it almost get your man Pete Cummins last Sunday?”
“What happened?”
“Pete was swimmin’ in the County River. Suddenly he felt somethin’ grab his leg. He said he put his head under the water to see what it was and what he saw scared the life outta him.”
“What did he see?”
“He said it was about ten feet long with a snake like body…like a Conger eel. It had a big head with big green eyes and instead of fins or flippers at the side, it had, like, big claws. He said its teeth were long and pointed…really ugly lookin’ thing.”
“There…see,” put in Po.
“And there’s supposed to be a big reward for anyone that catches it too,” added Red.
“A reward?” asked Dunno.
“Yeah, put up by the council I heard. They’re offerin’ £100.”
“Jasus,” gasped Dunno.
“So are ya comin’ with us?” asked Po.
“Too friggin’ right…£100…wow,” replied Dunno enthusiastically.

Later that afternoon the group of six were on their way walking the three mile hike to the river on the Rathfriland Road. The County River, as it was known locally, was an easy flowing water, over six feet deep in places which made it ideal for swimming and diving for the gang. Almost every weekend, when the weather was good, the boys made their way to the County for an afternoon of fun, football, swimming, sunbathing and keeping watchful eyes on the girls who turned up also.
Red and Po were at the back of the group.
“So what’s the plan?” whispered Red.

"All in hand…have the hose pipe in ma bag to breathe through."
"Will he fall for it?"
"Are ya kiddin'? He'll freak," laughed Po.
"He's pretendin' to be a big guy…very brave an all. He says it won't scare him," smiled Red.
"Yeah? We'll see how brave he is when the monster grabs him."

Thirty minutes later they were sitting on a grassy bank at the side of the County River just a few yards from a stone bridge. At this point the river was quite deep in the middle and had a sandy bottom which made it a nice place to bathe. When everyone was in the water with the usual splashing and complaints about the cold, Po winked at Red. He had the length of hose hidden under the water. Red moved beside Po who slipped him one end of the hose. After putting the other end in his mouth he gently submerged. Red kept his end of the hose behind his back and out of the water to enable Po to breathe. He was out of sight of Dunno, who was about six feet from him.
"Hi Dunno?" Red shouted.
"Yo."
"No monster yet?"
"It knows I'm here ya see. The monster slayer is here. It's hidin' somewhere shakin' with fear," laughed Dunno.
Po swam under the water towards Dunno. At this point it was about four feet deep. He reached out with both hands and grabbed Dunno's leg. Suddenly the expression on Dunno's face changed as did the colour. He had almost instantly gone very grey.
"Ahhh…," Dunno yelled. "Somethin's grabbed me."
"What is it Dunno?" Red shouted back pretending concern.
"I can't move, it's pullin' me…help me Red."
Red hurried to Dunno and made moves to try and drag him by the waist to the bank, now also being helped by Jumpy.
"Ahhh, it's pullin' me…"
Eventually, after a lot of tugging and pulling, Dunno's life was saved by Red and he was dragged safely onto the bank breathing heavily and in a state of shock. Po had now arrived on the scene and was helping the others make Dunno comfortable. He was laid on his back with a towel placed over him by Red.

"He looks bad Red…maybe ya should give him mouth to mouth," said Po trying hard not to laugh.
"Are ya outta your wee mind? He can die first," snapped Red.
"Jasus that was close Dunno," said Bishop. "Was it the monster?"
"Don't know…didn't see it," panted Dunno.
"It almost got ya Dunno…ya were very lucky ya know," added Po.
Dunno sat up slowly.
"It tried to drag me under ya know," he mumbled almost to himself.
"Why didn't ya grab it Dunno, sure ya could've went home with the reward."
"I'm lucky I'm goin' home with ma life so a am."
"Was it big?" asked Po.
"For sure it was…I could tell by the way it grabbed me…it was enormous."
"Jasus," said Red.
"Did anyone see it?" asked Jumpy.
"I saw a big round thing appear at the surface …then disappear again," said Bishop.
"That was Po's arse," whispered Red to Jumpy.

Dunno never again went swimming in the County River. He never forgot his close encounter with the River Monster and still tells the story of how he was close to being eaten alive. Red of course was the hero who without fear for his own life fought it off and got Dunno to safety. Later that night Red was awarded the 'Uncle Luigi's Café Special River Monster Bravery Award' by Anto who pinned the hand written award to his chest to much applause and cheering.

End

The Irish Dancing Class

1960

"No chance," said Red looking straight into Po's face.
"But Red…"
"No."
"But ya don't understand…"
"I do…and the answer is definitely…under no circumstances… never…not for any money…no!"
"Will I call for ya?"
"Are ya friggin' deef Po…I'm not goin'…and that's that."
"Seven o'clock then," said Po turning away as they reached the top of Mill Street.
"No…I'm warnin' ya…don't even think of callin' for me."

At seven fifteen that night Po and Red entered the back doors of 'The Bucket' on Castle Street.
"No…I'm not goin' in," mumbled Red.
Po grabbed him by the sleeve and dragged him the last few feet through the doors.
"Well, hello there boys. Have ya come to join with us?" came the soft lilting voice of Gerry Dorsey as he approached the boys.

"Oh Jasus," whispered Red.
Po kicked him on the shin and smiled sweetly.
"Hello Mr. Dorsey, yes we would like to join up. Red here has been torturing me to come."
Po met Red's eyes which were silently saying... 'Ya will die a death which will be slow and painful when I get ya outside'.
"Wonderful...wonderful. Have you ever done any Irish Dancing before then?"
"No, but Red always wanted to learn...didn't ya Red?" smiled Po.
"Couldn't wait," mumbled Red.
"Wonderful...wonderful. Now just sit yourselves down here and I will get one of the girls to get you started."

Mr. Dorsey hurried off in the direction of a group of girls at the other side of the hall.
"Are ya out of your tiny friggin' mind ya wee bastard?" Red snorted at Po.
"Don't worry, sure ya'll love it...just wait."
"Bad enough that Mr. Wonderful's as bent as a rubber penny, but he'll be wantin' us to wear skirts ya know."
"Will ya ever give ma head a bit a peace Red. In the first place they're not skirts, they're Irish dancin' kilts."
"They're friggin' skirts ta me so they are...Jasus if that Anto bastard finds out I'm here, I'll have ta leave Newry."
"Shush, here's somebody comin'."
A tall elegant girl in her early twenties approached Red and Po.
"Hello, my name's Marie Crogan. I'll get ya started over here with the beginner group. What's your names?"
"I'm Po Hillen and your man here's Red Morgan."
Marie shook hands with both and led them to the bottom of the hall where a small group of people were seated.
"Take a seat here and we'll get ya started in a few minutes," Marie smiled.

Red looked around as if looking for an escape route.
"Jasus, I'm getting ta hell outta here."
Po grabbed Red's coat forcing him down into the seat.
"Shush will ya."
"I'm finished, I'll never live this down. How in the name a God did I let ya talk me inta comin' here? I need ma friggin' head examined so a do."
"Look, it's only for a few classes so it is. I promised me ma."
"I know…but why?"
"Long story…tell ya later."
Red put his head in his hands and mumbled.
"Oh Christ…help me…please…I'll do anythin'…just get me outta here."
"Oh my God…there she is…Jasus…" whispered Po.
"There who is?"
"Joan," answered Po softly, his eyes fixed and glazed.
"Joan?"
"Over there in the blue dress."
"Joan Bannon?"
"Yeah…isn't she like a movie star?"
"So that's why I'm stuck here, ya got the hots for some friggin' chick."
"She's not some friggin' chick…she's a princess."
"Oh Jasus," Red returned his face to his hands.
"Look at the way she moves…elegant, feminine, graceful like."
"She moves well in bed too I hear."
"Who said that?" snapped Po.
"The Abbey Football Team."
Red winced from an elbow in the ribs.
"Now can we all line up please?" came the voice of a tall girl in a short green skirt.
"My name is Mary Sheridan. I will get ya all started on your introduction to Irish Dancin'."

An hour later Red and Po were descending the steps from The Bucket.
"It wasn't that hard was it?" said Po.
"Not too bad I suppose," mumbled Red reluctantly.
"Well, I think I could be good at it."
"Ya were all over the place for Christ sake."
"I was not…I was good…even Mary what's-her-name said so."
"She felt sorry for ya."
"Piss off."
"So tell me about this one ya are all in love with."
"Don't ya start now Morgan. I'm not in love with anybody…I just think she's lovely that's all."
"Yeah right…and it was your mom who made ya come here wasn't it?"
"Listen you, I told ya ma mom made me go and I had ta promise."
"Of course ya did."
"Well don't believe me then."
"I have no intention of believin' ya."
"Fine."
"Fine…but ya understand that this being serious news…about ya being in love and all…Anto will have ta be told…it's only right and proper ya know."
"Red…ya wouldn't tell that Anto bastard would ya?"
"Well after all, he's our mate…and he deserves ta know."
"He'll destroy me, I'll never hear the end of it…ya know what he's like."
"Anto? …the soul of discretion is Anto."
"Is he shit…he'd put up a sign in the shop so he would."
"A sign…now there's an idea…"
Po stopped and grabbed Red's arm.
"Ok bastard…what do ya want?"
"Po are ya sayin' that I…your bestest friend in the whole world would stoop ta blackmail?"
"Yeah, that's what I'm sayin'. Ok then…free chips for a week?"

"Don't know about that…"
"And the Pictures on Saturday?"
"Done."
"Done."

The relationship between best friends was a fragile thing that needed to be nourished and at times, paid for. Po, in the coming week would no doubt make it his mission to get something on Red and the deal would be renegotiated as had happened on numerous occasions in the past. Thus the balance of friendship would be again restored.

End

The Kite

1960

They were all gathered on the beach that Saturday in Warrenpoint, getting the new kite ready for its maiden flight. It was owned by Dunno and made by his father for him as a birthday present.
"This is the biggest kite I've ever seen," commented Red.
"That it is," added Po. "It must be six foot tall at least."
"Its six foot four tall and four foot across," boasted Dunno.
"But will it get off the ground Dunno?" asked Anto.
"Of course it will…sure isn't there a great wind today ta help it," replied Dunno.
"There's a strong wind all right, I hope ya'll be able ta hold her," commented Red.
"Don't worry, she'll fly to the clouds for sure," smiled Dunno.
"Right, that's everythin' ready now, she's ready ta go," said Jumpy standing up.
"Right Dunno, now you take the cord and head down the beach about twenty yards or so and we'll hold her up for the wind to catch her," said Red as he began lifting the kite which was green and white in colour, specially picked by Dunno, who was a supporter of Glasgow Celtic Football Club.

Warrenpoint beach was for the most part covered in stones. But there was one section of the beach that had a stretch of sand where the boys were usually to be found. The coast road was some ten feet above the beach and gave walkers and drivers alike a panoramic view of both the beach and the beautiful Carlingford Lough which lay between the graceful and sweeping Cooley Mountains on one side and the tall rolling Mournes on the other.

Dunno ran down the beach and the kite was lifted upright. The strong wind immediately caught it, lifted it off the ground and it climbed quickly into the summer sky. Dunno was controlling the cord and continued to unwind it, allowing the kite to gain more altitude.
"How's it feel?" shouted Red.
"She's...hard...to...hold," Dunno shouted back.
"Don't let go that cord Dunno...tie it around your wrist," added Anto.
Dunno seemed to be struggling with the cord but somehow got it around his wrist. He waved to the gang and held up his arm to show them everything was secure. The wind suddenly picked up strength and the kite began to move along the beach quite quickly. Dunno was having trouble holding it... he began running along the beach to keep up.
"I can't hold it," he managed to shout as he whizzed past his mates who had cleared a way for him.
"Jasus that thing is movin' Red," commented Po.
"Come on...we'd better get after him," Red shouted over his shoulder.
The whole gang raced after him along the beach shouting helpful things like, 'Don't let go,' and 'Hang on.'
"Shit...look," panted Red pointing in the direction of Dunno who was now being dragged. "It's headin' towards the sea."
The kite had turned with the wind direction and was indeed heading towards the sea taking the now helpless Dunno with it. He had tied the strong string to his wrist and could not now get it off to free himself. His feet were now dragging in the shallow water. Suddenly the kite turned again and was coming back towards the chasing posse.

"Try and grab him and hold on when he reaches us," shouted Red to the gang.
They did just that as Dunno arrived at speed screaming. They all grabbed at him but no one was able to get a firm hold except Po who managed to get hold of Dunno's trousers. Unfortunately Dunno's belt was unable to take the strain and by the time Po let go, his trousers and his underpants, were now around his ankles.

The flying Dunno had now become the focus of everyone on the beach as well as people walking on the promenade. Cars had begun to stop, spilling their occupants eager to see the great spectacle.
Eventually the kite crashed and Dunno came down quite hard on his backside skidding to a halt to the cheering and applause of his friends and watching public.

Later, back in Uncle Luigi's, poor Dunno was taking the usual teasing about flying around Warrenpoint beach naked from the waist down.
"Well at least ya can say that every woman in Warrenpoint has seen your wee willie."
"Jasus, don't remind me."
"This is true," added Red. "Ya'll be the talk of the town."
"It might even reach the papers ya know," put in Po. "There were people with cameras there…a mean, it's not every day ya see a wee wrinkled thing like that flying around Warrenpoint beach."

The teasing of Dunno was unrelenting. No attempt was made in any way to spare poor Dunno's blushes. Finally Anto stood up…
"I have to start work now, bye flasher…" he smiled back at Dunno. He stopped, turned and came back to the snug. "Ya know lads, from this day on, Dunno's escapade on the beach will be known as 'The Day of the Flying Willie'."

And so it was. Dunno became immortalised from that day forth.

Poetic Justice

1960

"I got warned about it this mornin'," grumbled Po.
"What did she say?" asked Red.
"Well, I was reminded that dad is up for a promotion on the buses this year and that Shitface's da is the one that will have the decision ta promote him. If a bash that sneaky wee bastard and he tells his da, it could be bad all round."
Red and Po were sitting in Uncle Luigi's sipping Coke.
"Ok, now let me get this straight, this 'Shitface' as ya call him, Pokey Harrison, whose da happens ta be your da's boss, gave your Paul a hidin' after school, givin' him a bloody nose and a black eye, am I right?"
"Yeah."
"Now Shitface, I am thinkin', is a lot bigger than your fella, and about four years older, right?"
"Yeah."
"And, you're not allowed ta kick the shit outta him?"
"Right."
"Not good a'tall a'tall."
"I have ta smile at the creep, can ya believe it? I can do nothin', say nothin' and can't touch him."

Anto arrived at the snug and sat down drying his hands on a towel. Red told him the whole story word for word.
"Holy shit, ya know, I'm glad I'm not in your shoes Po, I'm not sure a could keep ma hands off the whore."
"Ya know Po, over the years ya have come up with some brilliant ideas for gettin' people back that gave us shit. Are ya now sayin' that when somebody stomps on your toes ya can do nothin' about it?" pointed out Red.
"He's right ya know Po. If we ever needed ta get someone, we always left it ta yourself ta come up with an idea," added Anto seriously.
"I can come up with plenty of ideas all right, but they all include killin' him."
"Look, just think about it for a few days, somethin' will pop into your brain, like, it's not as if there's no room," smiled Red. This just got him a kick under the table that made him wince.

A week passed and the incident was not mentioned again. Red was in his back garden, weeding the vegetable patch for his granny when Po arrived. He was grinning from ear to ear. Red looked up and smiled.
"Don't tell me, wee Danna Mullins let ya kiss her."
"No."
"She didn't?"
"I never tried ta kiss her."
"You should never take up lyin' as a profession, ya'd starve ta death."
"Will ya shut up will ya, I've got it."
"Off Danna Mullins?"
"Jasus will ya listen, I got an idea to get that bastard that hit our fella."
"The Pokey Harrison bastard are ya talkin' about?"
"The very same bastard."
"Ya come up with a plan have ya?"
"I have, and a bloody good one too."
"Well now, this calls for a mug of tay an jam butties for sure," smiled Red putting down his spade.

They both went to the kitchen which was empty. Red made the tea and Po, the jam butties. When they were seated, Red was the first to speak.
"Ok then, so let's hear it."
"Well ya see it hit me an hour ago when a was talkin' ta Jumpy Jones down the town. He was tellin' me he was talkin' ta Shitface Harrison. Now, as it happens, they don't play Kaddy on his estate ya see, so he was askin' Jumpy about the rules."
"I see, a think, so he wants ta learn Kaddy, why?"
"Knowin' him, he'll want ta show off ta the boys on his estate."
"Ok, I can see that."
"That's when the idea hit me."
"Go on."
"A told Jumpy ta tell him that I would be delighted ta show him the finer points of the game as I was the best at it in the town of Newry."
"Are ya indeed?"
"Shut up will ya, a just told Jumpy ta tell him that, so he'd ask me ta teach him."
"Ok, so, ya want to teach Shitface to play Kaddy. Po, a have ta tell ya, that's for sure one of your great ideas," laughed Red.
"Don't be a smart arse you, wait till ya hear the whole plan."
Ten minutes later Po had dragged Red onto the street.
"Now, go an knock Mrs. McNulty's door and see if she is in?"
"Why?"
"Just do it, if she is, just ask her does she want any messages or somethin'."
Red followed Po's instructions, more from curiosity than desire.
"Ok, no one home, now what?"
"Did ya bring the Kaddy?"
"Yeah, have it here."
"Right, I'll start. I'll hit off from over there."
"Ya can't play there, we're not allowed. Mrs. McNulty got her window broke with a Kaddy and we're not allowed to play here anymore."
"I know," said Po slyly. "Now go over there and stand in front of McNulty's window."
Red did so.

"Now make sure ya catch this, right?"
"Right, right."

The Kaddy was a six inch length of square wood, tapered to a point at both ends. Each side was marked with a number, one through four. The Kaddy was placed on the edge of the footpath and struck with a small bat or stick. As the Kaddy rose in the air it was struck a second time as far as possible. When it landed, which ever number on the Kaddy was facing up, the player had that number of jumps to get to where the Kaddy started. If he succeeded, the player who was at the 'bat' was out. If the Kaddy was caught, the player at 'bat' was out. The game would continue until all the team batting were out.

Po laid the Kaddy on the edge of the footpath. He hit it with his stick and the Kaddy went straight for Red who caught it easily. Po did it five more times and each time Red caught it. They returned to Red's house for more tea.
"Ya got the whole plan yet?" Po asked as he sat down at the table.
"Ta be honest ya lost me halfway through."
Po laughed loudly.
"Now ya noticed that ya caught the Kaddy right in front of the window, right?"
"Right."
"Now what de ya think might happen if ya weren't there?"
"It would go through the window of course, Jasus, I've got it, you're gonna get Shitface ta hit the Kaddy, right?"
"Right."
"Holy shit, he'll be up ta his neck in it for sure," laughed Red.
"And ta just complete the plan, we have ta make sure Mrs. McNulty is home. I'll stand in front of the door, I measured it already, and the bell would be just behind ma head. Just before he hits the Kaddy I'll lean against the bell, get it?"
"I get it, herself will be on her way ta the door as the Kaddy goes through the window."
"Correct and right, your front door will be open, so, by the time she opens her door I'll be in your house and Shitface will be standin' on his own with his big mouth wide open," laughed Po.

****

Anto got thirty minutes off work to be there. He said to Red, that this was something he did not want to miss. Po had been, as expected, asked by Pokey Harrison to teach him to play Kaddy. Po had spent twenty minutes showing him how to hold the bat and hit the Kaddy in the safety of the St. Clare's Convent field.
"Ya know, a think ya have it Pokey. Now it's time ta try your skills on the street, come on," said Po heading for Castle Street.
"Right, I'll go across the road and see if a can catch it."
Po went straight to his predetermined spot where he had made a secret mark on the footpath.
He looked along the street and noted Red and Anto casually leaning on a windowsill at Red's house. They both waved at Po, who smiled, and turned to face Pokey who was waiting to start.
"Right Pokey, off ya go."
As the bat was on its way to the Kaddy, Po leaned his head on Mrs. McNulty's bell. As per expectation the Kaddy headed straight for the window. A moment later there was a loud shattering sound as Mrs. McNulty's front window disintegrated into a thousand pieces. Po was already on his way to Red's house. Both Anto and Red were already inside. Po raced breathlessly through the door where he met his two laughing friends. Po placed a finger in front of his mouth indicating the boys to be quiet. Outside they could hear the loud high pitched screaming voice of Mrs. McNulty and the low bewildered, painfully apologetic voice of Pokey.

The following day it was learned that Pokey's father had to pay for the window replacement. Pokey was grounded for a week, lost his pocket money for three months, and got a 'hiding' from both his mom and dad, plus he was told under pains of more punishment, he was never again to play Kaddy.

"A have ta tell ya Po, a job well done. One of your best yet a have to say, what do ya think Red?" said Anto.
"Have ta agree, it was a beauty for sure."

"Well, sure it wasn't all that hard when a put ma mind to it," said Po smugly as he crossed his arms and looked up at the ceiling.
"Oh my God, he's off again," sighed Red putting his face in his hands.
Anto began laughing.
"So what'll we call this one then Po?"
"Well now, let's see, how about Poetic Justice?"
Anto and Red held up their coffee mugs.
"Poetic Justice," they said in unison.

End

The Haunted House

1960

"No way, I'm not goin', you're nuts," complained Red.
"It'll be the best a craic," smiled Po.
"For who? I don't think so."
"Ach Red, come on. If ya don't go, I won't go."
"So, don't go then."
"But I was lookin' forward ta it so a was."
"We'll get fish an chips in Uncle Luigi's. Better for ya anyway."
"Ah Red, look at all the favours a done for ya. I came up with excuses ta get ya out a trouble with your da on hundreds of occasions. I even went against my principles and told lies for ya. Not ta mention the time ya were in trouble with your one from Dromalane, the blond with the legs. Then there was that thing over the stolen apples in the market where I…"
"All right, all right, all right. Jasus, you're worse than an auld doll the way ya nag."
Po didn't answer, just smiled. He knew he could get around Red. All he had to do was keep on at him and surrender would be imminent.
"All right, I'll friggin' go, anythin' ta get ya off me."

"Sure you're just a great human being and a wonderful footballer. If ya were only that wee bit better lookin' then ya would be on the same level as ma own self."
"Jasus help me," moaned Red to Po's amusement.

Red, Po, Jumpy and Anto had reached Monaghan Street before Red spoke.
"Well, what's the story with this house?" he asked Po.
"There was this auld lady that lived there, a Mrs. Duey I think she was from Dundalk originally. Anyways, she was ancient, like in her seventies. One day someone called ta see her and found her hangin' from a rope. She had been dead for nearly a week. Since that day on, neighbours say they have heard strange noises and two even claim ta have seen her lookin' out the window."
"They were probably drunk," added Anto.
"No they weren't. These two didn't drink. My mom knows them," replied Po.
"So when did this all happen then?" asked Jumpy.
"About two years ago. They tried to sell the house but no one wanted ta live in it," said Po.
"I wouldn't fancy livin' in a house where someone hanged themselves either," added Jumpy.
"So we're gonna see the ghost and stuff?" Red asked Po sarcastically.
"We mightn't see anythin' a'tall…and then again…we might," said Po making his voice deeper.
"Ya do know that if we are caught breakin' in ta this house we'll be in serious shit?" put in Red in a serious tone.
"I've already been there and taken care of everythin'," smiled Po.
"What did ya do?" asked Anto.
"I got in the back window and took the bar off the back door, so we just have ta walk in."
"We could still get caught," complained Red.
"Will ya stop with the moanin' Morgan. We won't get caught. Remember everybody, no talkin', no noise a'tall…right?" said Po seriously to everyone.
They soon reached Edward Street and turned up into a little cul-de sac named McGuiness Street.

"Which one is it?" asked Anto.
"Number 70, over there with the brown door," answered Po.
"Now you guys wait here, I'll go round the back and get in and open the front door," continued Po.
Five minutes later the front door was opened and everyone was inside.
"So what do we do now?" asked Red looking at Po in the dim light coming from the street.
"Well, now we get comfortable and just wait."
"And if this ghost turns up, what do we say ta him or her? Hello, my name's Anto, de ya want me ta get ya some chips?"
This got a giggle from all.

There was an old sofa and two armchairs in the living room. The house had a damp, stuffy sort of smell that was unpleasant to say the least. The boys all sat down and made themselves as comfortable as possible on the living room seating.
"What time is it?" whispered Jumpy.
"Eleven thirty," answered Anto.
"How long do we have ta wait?" asked Red.
"How the hell do I know, for Christ sake Red, we wait until the ghost turns up," complained Po.
"Maybe it's off haunting somewhere else," added Anto.
"Frig me Anto, ya know nothin' about ghosts do ya? Ghosts stay where they die ya ejit, everybody knows that," sneered Po.
"Jasus, am awful sorry for not knowin' the habits of ghosts Po. I've never talked ta one ya see."
"Smart arse," mumbled Po. "Anyway, will ya all shut up will ya? We need ta be quiet or it won't appear."
"This place is givin' me the willies," whispered Jumpy.
"Shut up," came the response from the other three.

Shortly after midnight Red was laid back on an armchair with his eyes closed thinking about his girlfriend Maureen, who he was planning to see on Friday. He smiled when he thought of her reaction when he related to her the story of where they were tonight.

Suddenly there was a noise from the room above, like a floorboard creaking. Then it happened again, louder this time.
"Shit, did ya hear that?" whispered Jumpy.
"Shush," said Po. "Listen."
Everything was silent…too silent. In the dim light Red saw Jumpy making the sign of the cross.
Again came the creak, and again. They were sure now. It was the sound of something moving across the bedroom floor above.
"There's somethin' up there for friggin' sure," whispered Anto.
"I think we should get outta here," said Jumpy with a hint of panic in his voice.
"No, we have ta wait, I wanna see it so I do," said Po.
"Well I don't," said Anto standing up.
Now the noise was on the landing. It was definitely a footstep. It began to very slowly descend the stairs.
"I'm gettin' ta hell outta here," said Jumpy.
Everyone was on their feet now and heading for the living room door. Red was first there followed by Anto, Jumpy next with Po last.
There was a small stool lying on its side in the hall. Both Red and Anto had stepped over it but Jumpy didn't see it and tripped, landing on the floor with Po on top of him. Red and Anto were by this time at the bottom of the street. They stopped running when they reached Monaghan Street and looked back. Po and Jumpy were racing toward them. When they arrived both were pale and shaking.
"We saw her, Jasus we saw her…didn't we Po?"
Po couldn't speak. He was leaning on his knees trying to breathe. He just nodded. They walked slowly back to Uncle Luigi's talking about what had happened. Both Po and Jumpy had by now got their breath back and couldn't be shut up.
"Well, when I was gettin' up from the floor I looked up the stairs… Jasus, ya would not believe what a saw," panted Jumpy.
"What?" asked a serious Anto.
"Her."
"Her?" repeated Red.
"Yeah, her. Jumpy's right. I saw her too," said Po. "The old lady who hung herself. She was standin' halfway down the stairs…all glowin' so she was."

Jumpy hit Po with the back of his hand on the arm.
"Tell them about the noose."
"She had a rope around her neck…I swear on my grannies grave she had."
"Jasus," said Red and Anto together looking at each other.
"I'm sure glad I didn't see that," said Anto to Red.
"Me too. I think I would have fainted on the spot," said Red in a serious voice.

Ten minutes later they were all back at the café, seated in the front snug drinking Coke and going over again every second of the ghostly apparition. Topcoat arrived with Martina Carroll from the back of the café. Martina was a tall girl who worked in the café at weekends and was a good friend of Anto.
Anto stood up and spoke to Martina. "Did ya see the amount of fish Uncle Luigi got today?"
"Naw, was it a lot?"
"Come out the back ta ya see."
Anto and Martina left the group.
"Tell Topcoat about tonight," said Red to Po, "I'll be back in a minute."
Red found Anto and Martina laughing loudly out the back of the café.
"Well?" asked Red as he arrived.
"Friggin' perfect wasn't it?" laughed Anto.
"That it was, but I was disappointed I didn't get ta see the old lady."
"She was friggin' perfect. I saw her just before she left here with Topcoat. Jasus, sure your man Cecil B.DeMille couldn't have had her made up better, wig, wrinkles and all. Ask Topcoat, sure she looked about a hundred years old for sure," laughed Anto. "And…the idea of Topcoat lying on the landin' with the torch shinin' on her back makin' her glow was a touch of genius, even if I do say so my own self. Martina, ya should get an Academy Award so ya should," laughed Anto.
"There, ya see Anto, and you always slaggin' me off for bein' in the Newry Players Drama Group. The stage make-up, it sure came in handy tonight," laughed Martina.

"It did for sure, but my idea of the noose was good too don't forget and even better was the leaving of the stool for Po and Jumpy to fall over," laughed Red.
"A have ta admit that was a touch of pure greatness Red. What put it in your mind anyways?"
"I was thinkin' that when we were all running out of the house, the boys might not have looked up the stairs and missed the whole thing, whereas, if they were ta fall down, well the chances were well improved," smiled Red.
"That was a brilliant idea for sure," laughed Martina.
"Now, we have to be very careful that neither Jumpy nor Po find out it was us," whispered Anto.
"Too right," said Red. "Knowin' Po, he'll spend the rest of his life tryin' ta get his own back."

So the legend of the hanged lady became part of Newry's folklore. Po and Jumpy proudly tell the story to this day of their unwavering nerve and bravery in the face of the ghost of the hanging lady.

End

The Holy Well

1960

Red and Po were walking across the Ballybot Bridge in Newry that Friday when Po suddenly stopped.
"I knew I had somethin' to tell ya about."
"What now?" asked Red.
"Do ya remember last year when we were at the Mass Rock Procession?"
"Sure, don't we have ta go every year under pain of death or worse, from the wrinkly mob."
"I know, I know. Every year we walk that long three miles in the procession to Ballyholland and Mass Rock."

Mass Rock was the name given to a large flat topped granite rock in a field in Ballyholland, high above Newry. There were hundreds of these rocks dotted all over Ireland. They bear silent witness to times when Roman Catholics, their religion suppressed and churches confiscated and burned by the British King, held secret services during the 17th and 18th centuries at 'mass rocks' in the open air. Being caught at one of these secret religious services could cost worshippers their lives and on more than one occasion, did.

"I know, I know. Don't I have ta go ta the mass there every year Po. Why are ya tellin' me all this stuff?"
"Will ya listen, will ya?" went on Po undeterred.
"It's not as if I have a choice is it?" mumbled Red.
"Well, de ya remember last year I said I had the beginnin's of an idea about the well on Courtney Hill?"
"Sort of."
"I've worked it out and we can come outta this well ahead," smiled Po.
"There's a catch here, isn't there? And a have a feelin' it involves me, right?"
"Not a catch exactly, but wait till a tell ya the plan, sure ya'll love it."
By this time they had reached the Mall and were sitting on the wall that ran its length alongside the Clanrye River.
"You're nuts, cuckoo, crazy, out of your head," said Red pointing his finger at Po's face.
"Just think about it, it will work, I'm tellin' ya."
"The Pope will put a contract out on us."
"Nobody will know for Christ's sake, just you and me," said Po, still smiling.
"And you're sure about this?"
"Positive, definite, no problem."
"I'll think about it, that's all I'll say now, but I want ta hear all the details, every single one. Deal?"
"Deal."

****

It was Sunday and hundreds of people had gathered after twelve o'clock mass at Newry Cathedral for the annual procession to Mass Rock. Po and Red were there dressed in their Sunday suits making sure they were at the head of the crowd, right behind the priests. The procession began and followed the usual route along Hill Street, turning left into William Street, then through Abbey Yard past the Christian Brothers School and began the long climb up Courtney Hill. Near the top of Courtney Hill Po elbowed Red and they began to slow down slightly and move to the left. They stopped at a small well at the side of the

road at the top of Courtney Hill. The well was quite shallow and had three steps down to the water. The spring water was clear, about twelve inches deep with the bottom covered in small pebbles. There was just enough space for one person to use the well at a time because of the narrow width of the steps. Po took a position on the first step and began praying as loudly as he could without sounding as if he was shouting. "In the name of the Father, the Son and the Holy Ghost, Amen. Hail Mary full of grace........"
Red joined in at this point praying as loud as Po. They soon noticed others in the procession had stopped, lined up behind them, and began joining in. When three Hail Mary's and an Our Father had been said, Po reached into his pocket and made a big deal of making the sign of the cross again and throwing a coin into the well. Red did exactly the same. They then moved off to catch up again with the head of the procession. The crowd who had joined them began to follow suit and as Red and Po walked away, they could hear the splashes of coins going into the water. They could also hear the voices of those who had just begun to join the crowd at the well and were copying the prayers they had heard. They even heard some people asking, 'What prayers do we say?' Others telling them with some authority, as if they had been doing it for years.

Later that evening, just before dark, Red and Po returned to the well and began the task of retrieving the coins. Po had taken a large empty paint tin for the task. The coin retrieval took longer than expected because of the fact that the entrance steps were so narrow that only one person could fit on them. They duly finished however and returned to Po's house well laden with the tin of heavy coins.
"Well?"
"Wait a minute will ya," snapped Po.
"So, how much?"
"Eleven pounds, eleven shillin's an three pence, plus five medals, and two washers."
"Jasus," gulped Red. "A don't believe it."
"Didn't a tell ya it would be a great idea?"
"Eleven. Nearly twelve quid, it's unbelievable."
"Uncle Luigi's for a fish supper?" inquired Po.

"Let's go."
"Now not a word about this ta anyone, not even Anto, right?" said Po seriously.
"Agreed."
"We can do this every year ya know," smiled Po.
"Sure ya'r a wee genius person, no mistake," laughed Red
"True, true," smiled Po polishing his finger nails on his jumper.
A short time later the two were seated alone in a snug in Uncle Luigi's Café.
Po lifted his bottle of Coke.
"A toast," he smiled.
Red lifted his bottle.
"Ta the only collection the church will never get its hands on," laughed Po.
"And ta our Holy Mother Church without who we would be broke tonight and not even be able ta go ta the Pictures. Ya know if we were Prods we wouldn't have holy wells and stuff ya know, so, God save the Pope," added Red.
"God save the wee man and his red cotton socks," agreed Po as they clinked bottles.

End

The Gas Men

1960

That Tuesday evening Red, Po, Anto and Topcoat Anderson were sitting in the first snug at Uncle Luigi's. The discussion in progress was about a serious incident which happened the evening before involving Dunno and Jumpy.

"And they're both in hospital?" Red asked Po, who, as usual, appeared to have the most up to date information on what was going on.
"Them two ejits are always in trouble," laughed Anto. "Now it's gas meters, what next?"
"Did I ever tell ya the story that happened durin' the war here in the town about a gas meter?" asked Topcoat. Everyone shook their heads.
"Well, ya see when the German planes were goin' ta bomb the shipyards and stuff in Belfast they used ta come over Newry on their way to and from their targets. Ya see, the South was a neutral country and they couldn't get attacked there by the RAF, which, as ya know, is only three miles from here. Anyway, sometimes when they were comin' back from a raid on Belfast, they might not have been able ta get rid of all their bombs. Now ya see, the weight of the bombs would have slowed them down, especially if they were bein' chased by the RAF, so they would get

rid of them anywhere they could and Newry would have been as good a place as any ta drop them. So what they would do here is sound the sirens ta let everyone know they were comin' over. The people used ta grab what they could carry and head for the nearest hill, which at this side of the town would've been Courtney Hill. These two guys were walkin' up the hill and saw this old lady strugglin' ta push her pram. They offered to help her and pushed this pram all the way to the top of the hill. When they got there they were wrecked, cause the pram wasn't light. One of them remarked that through all the noise and confusion the baby never wakened. He pulled back the blanket and there lying in the pram, as nice as ya please was your auld ones gas meter."
"What did your auld one say?" laughed Anto.
"Well, ya didn't expect me ta leave ma meter in the house for somebody ta come in an rob it did ya?"
There was a round of prolonged laughter from everyone there.

"Right now, Po. Get back ta Jumpy and Dunno will ya?"
"Where was I? Oh yeah, well the story I got came from Dunno's sister, who went to see him in hospital this morning."
"Well, how bad are they?" asked Anto, who was standing at the table in his apron. He was working tonight in his uncle's café but did not want to miss the up to date gossip about last night's incident.
"From what I hear, Dunno has a few cuts on his face and is badly bruised and has a broken ankle. Jumpy has a few bruises too and a broken arm. They might be gettin' out today."
"Them two don't have a brain cell between them ya know," Red commented.
"I only know bits and pieces of the story, so, start from the beginin' Po and tell us what happened," said Topcoat.
"Well, I was talkin' to them yesterday in here. They were headin' up ta McCoy's old house in North Street. The McCoys got a new house up in Derrybeg so they did, anyway the boys were intendin' ta get in the back of the house ta see if there was anything left they could sell. So, they got in and were lookin' about when Jumpy spotted that the gas meter was still there. They tried to get it disconnected but could only get one of the pipes loosened. They had to go home ta get some tools

ta do the job. When they returned it was almost dark and they got back to work on the meter."

"Why didn't they just break open the friggin' lock, a mean what did they want with the whole friggin' meter?" asked Topcoat.

"Topcoat, ya have ta remember, this is Dunno and Jumpy we're talkin' about here," put in Red.

"True, true, forgot about that," laughed Topcoat.

"Did they get the meter out then?" asked Anto.

"Ah, well, now we come ta the interestin' bit," answered Po taking another sip of his Coke.

"Will ya get on with the story for Christ's sake. It takes ya that long, you're worse than an auld one," snapped Red impatiently.

"Will ya hold your horses will ya? I'm goin' as fast as a can."

"Well go on then, a have ta get back ta work sometime taday," complained Anto.

"Yous are such smart arses aren't ya. Well, they were workin' on the second pipe when Jumpy said he was gettin' a strong smell of gas. Dunno said he could smell it too."

"Was the pipe broke?" asked Topcoat.

"Will ya wait will ya? Anyway, Dunno decided to have a look ta see if he could see where the gas was comin' from ya see. They had no torch, so can ya guess what Dunno did?"

"No...no way, a know he's stupid but surely he's not that dumb?" said Red with a look of amazement on his face. Po just smiled and nodded.

"Jasus Christ," put in Anto.

"Will yous frigger's tell me what the hell happened? Did a miss somethin' or what?" asked Topcoat.

"Look, ya have two geniuses together in a room filled with gas, it's dark, they can't see anythin', they have no torch, so what de ya think Dunno and Jumpy would do?"

Topcoat thought for a moment, then his face changed. He looked across to Red and then at Anto.

"Naw...no way...Naw, they couldn't be that stupid."

Po just nodded his head again. "Stupid would be puttin' it mildly. Didn't Dunno only light a match and the whole place went up."

"They were lucky they weren't killed," added Anto.

"That's for sure," agreed Red.

"Well," said Po sitting back and folding his arms. "Ya know what this is don't ya?"

"What."

"The Brainless twins will go down in Newry history as the idiots who went lookin' for a gas leak with a match," laughed Po.

"Or how about the quickest way to open a gas meter," put in a smiling Topcoat.

"No, I have it," said Anto. The newspaper headlines will read, "The theory of gas flight proven in Newry."

End

The Orchard Revenge

1960

Jumpy and Dunno had just reached the six foot wall surrounding McGinn's house and orchard on the Ballyholland Road. As per the plan, Dunno gave Jumpy a leg up. When he reached the top of the wall, he straddled it and began to pull his mate Dunno up.
"Will ya look at the size of them apples on the top of that tree," whispered Jumpy.
"I see them, friggin' monsters aren't they?" answered Dunno.
"Come on," said Jumpy as he dropped into McGinn's orchard.
A few minutes later the boys were filling their bag with the largest apples they could get off the trees. The biggest ones however were a little higher up, out of reach.
"We have ta get them ones up there, look at them will ya?" puffed Dunno pointing up the tree.
"Keep the bag open as wide as ya can," answered Jumpy as he began to shake the tree.
Apples began to rain down on top of Dunno who of course stopped quite a number of them with his head. Dunno cried out in pain and dropped his bag.

"Ya friggin' ejit," he shouted at Jumpy who was laughing at his friend's misfortune.
"Hi, what are ya doin' there?" came a loud voice from the direction of McGinn's house.
The two took off at speed towards the wall. They used the same technique as when entering with Dunno giving Jumpy a leg up. This time however when Dunno was being pulled up by Jumpy Mr. McGinn had arrived and had a firm grip on Dunno's leg. It took a lot of kicking and wriggling for Dunno to get his leg free, which, he eventually did, unfortunately, less one shoe. They were almost into the town centre before they stopped running.
"Friggin' auld bastard," complained Dunno.
"Friggin' auld bastard is right, we'll get our revenge on him so we will," puffed Jumpy when they stopped to catch their breath.

They eventually reached Uncle Luigi's where they found Red, Po and the Bishop sitting in the first snug. Red looked up at Dunno who was carrying a shoe in one hand.
"I know this might be a stupid question, but why are ya in your stockin' soles and carryin' a shoe?"

Between the two of them the story was related in great detail to the seated group who were at this stage well into sustained laughter.
"I know this might be yet another stupid question and I will probably be sorry I asked Dunno, but why are ya carryin' that shoe? A mean, are ya hopin' ta find a match for it?"
This made the group laugh even more.
"We will find a way ta get our own back on that auld McGinn bastard so we will, just ya wait and see," said Dunno annoyed at the continued laughter from his friends. Po looked at Red.
"Did ya hear that Red? Dunno's gonna get his own back. He's lookin' for his shoe."
This brought on the laughter once again to both Dunno and Jumpy's annoyance. They just gave the group a finger sign and left.

A few days later Red and Po were helping out with the cleaning at closing time at the café, when Dunno and Jumpy arrived both looking pleased with themselves.

"Well will ya look who it isn't," smiled Po.
"Well lads can we give ya a hand?" asked Dunno.
"Grab a mop there lads," said Anto. "We're near finished anyway."
Ten minutes later they were all seated in the first snug eating fish and chips.
"So why are you two lookin' so pleased with yourselves?" asked Red.
"Sure didn't we only get our own back on that auld McGinn fella," smiled Jumpy.
"Ya did?" said Anto. "This should be good," he laughed, looking at Red and Po.
"Go on then, tell us, and don't leave out a word."
"Well, I have ta be honest," said Dunno.
"That'll make a change," put in Po.
"Very funny, will ya listen will ya? It was all Jumpy's idea so it was."
"Will ya get on with it for God's sake and tell us," complained Anto.
"Jumpy remembered that auld McGinn had a load of turkeys," Dunno stopped to allow himself a giggle. "He remembered some Christmas stuff his parents had in the attic and went up and got it. We went back to McGinn's and climbed up on the wall at the end where the turkeys were kept. We both at the same time popped up wearin' Father Christmas hats."
Both Dunno and Jumpy burst out laughing at what they had done. Red, Anto and Po sat looking at each other.
"Hang on Dunno, I think we missed somethin' here. You wore Santa Claus hats, right?" asked Red.
"Yeah, don't ya get it?"
"We're just a wee bit slow us lot. Will ya explain to us again what the hell you're talkin' about?"
Jumpy looked at Dunno.
"Jasus, ya know they are slow, aren't they?" he laughed.
"Ya better explain it ta them bunch of dopes Dunno."
"Look, can ya not put it together? When the turkeys looked up they saw the Santa hats, right?"
"Right," all three answered together.
"Well, so what happens ta turkeys at Christmas ya dopes?" laughed Dunno. "It scared the shit outta them, they were all runnin' around

the place like crazy, screechin' and screamin'. I'll bet they kept that auld McGinn frigger and his family up all night," put in a smiling Jumpy.
Red looked at Anto and Po. No one spoke for a full ten seconds. Then the whole place erupted.
Jumpy and Dunno joined in the laughter thinking of course that their three friends were laughing at their great stunt. They didn't understand that the boys were in fits at the stupidity of the whole story.
"I get it now Jumpy," roared Po. "The turkeys thought it was Christmas."
"That's it," agreed Jumpy.
Po lowered himself onto the floor.
"No, I can't take it, I can't take any more."
Anto just couldn't speak at all and Red was turning a very dangerous purple colour trying to breathe.

From that day forth Dunno and Jumpy became known as the 'Turkey Terrorists'.

End

Po the Cowboy

1960

Red was sitting on the footpath outside his house on Castle Street chatting to his best friend Po. He looked up and saw Michael McDonnell approaching. Michael worked for the nuns of the Poor Clare's as a sort of farm manager. They owned some land in Ballyholland on which they kept about ten cattle. During the summer Red would go with Michael in the mornings in the pony and trap to help milk the cows and let them out into the fields. In the evenings he would go back, help round up the cows, milk them again and lock them up for the night.

"Well boys."
"Hello Mr. McDonnell," answered Red and Po in unison.
"Red, I have run into a problem tonight and need ya ta do a favour for me."
"Sure, what is it?"
"I have ta take Mary to the hospital. I think her arm is broken. Stupid girl fell off a swing."
"So ya want me ta do the cows then?"
"Will ya be able ta manage on your own?"

"Sure a will, Po here is a dab hand with cows and he would love ta come and give me a hand. Wouldn't ya Po?"
"Yeah, can't wait," Po answered dryly.
"Here's the keys for the barn. Make sure everything is locked up tight. When you're finished milkin' just put the kegs in the wee room at the back of the barn, they'll be cool enough there till the mornin'."
"No problem."
"Thanks Red, I owe ya one, bye."
"Tell wee Mary I was askin' for her and a hope she's ok," said Red.
"I will," said Michael over his shoulder.

****

"Jasus, I never milked a stupid cow in my life so a didn't," moaned Po as Red and he were on their way up High Street later that evening.
"There's nothin' to it. Ya see ya just hold its tail and move it up and down like a pump and the milk goes straight into the keg for ya."
"Would ya ever piss off, I'm not that stupid ya know."
"Oh, sure a nearly forgot. I thought a saw your woman yesterday mornin' in Ballyholland when a was on my way ta milk the cows."
"My woman? Where?"
"In the next field to the Nuns."
"No way, my woman wouldn't be out there."
"I know, it was when a got closer I realised."
"Ya realised what?"
"It wasn't her a'tall so it wasn't. It was another cow altogether."
This got Red a punch.
"Hi Red…Po," came the high pitched voice of Roda Fitzpatrick. She was a pretty girl with long black hair and olive skin, and enormous brown eyes. With her was Ann O'Hanlon, another very good looking girl who had curly blond hair, blue eyes and what seemed like a permanent smile on her face. Lastly, was Tanda Crimmins, who was the comic of the three, forever playing jokes on and teasing the boys that lived in her area.
"Hi girls," answered Red. "What ya all up ta?"
"Just headin' into the town, where are ya goin'?" asked Tanda.
"Goin' to put the cows ta bed up at the Nuns."

"Just the two of ya?"
"Well, just me really. Ya see Po's afraid of cows ever since that time one winked at him."
Everyone laughed except Po who had begun to gain a little colour on his face.
"Don't listen ta him girls, de ya know how ya can tell when Red's tellin' lies?"
"How?" smiled Roda.
"When his lips are movin'."
This got Po a round of laughter from the girls.
"Did I ever tell ya about the time he fell in cow shit down the Warrenpoint Road?"
"Po, we have ta hurry, its gettin' dark."
"You're not goin' anywhere till I hear the story," said Roda grabbing Po's arm.
"Well, it's like this ya see. We were messin' around in Daly's field when your man tripped over himself and ended up with his face in the biggest mound of cow shit ya ever seen."
At this the girls burst into laughter once again pointing at Red and holding their noses. Red leaned over to Po grabbing his arm.
"See you small stuff, you're dead, stone cold dead."
Po just laughed and stuck his tongue out.

Fifteen minutes later the boys arrived at the Nun's fields.
"Now, de ya know what a cow looks like?" asked Red.
"You're a real comedian aren't ya Morgan?"
"Well just in case, they have a leg at each corner ta sort a balance themselves. At the back ya'll see a tail so you'll know the head's at the other end."
"Very funny ya whore, now what do we have ta do first?" asked Po.
"We have ta get the cows inta the barn first."
"How de ya do that?"
"Just watch."
Red went into the barn and emerged with a galvanised bucket and a small shovel. He began banging the side of the bucket with the shovel and the cows at the other end of the field looked up and began to hurry in the direction of the barn, all except one.

"Brilliant," exclaimed Po. "But what about the other one?"
"That's Jenny, she's a real stuck up bitch that one."
"How do we get her in then?" asked Po seriously.
"Well now, this is the difficult one ya see. It takes a bit of fine cunning."
"Why don't we do it like the Cowboys do, ya know, lasso her?"
"Are ya serious?"
"Of course. I could lasso her and lead her in. Have ya a rope?"
"There's one hanging up in the barn I think."
Po went into the barn and emerged a few moments later swinging a rope above his head.
"Head em up, move em out," sang Po.
"You're goin' ta do it?"
"No bother ta this Cowboy."
"Ok. Go right on ahead then."
Without a word Po headed off, skipping across the field in the direction of Jenny pretending he was on a horse. Jenny was eating grass at the far end of the field totally unconcerned. When he reached Jenny she just lifted her head and looked at him. Po slipped the rope over her head without any problem.
"Hi Po, make sure ya wrap the rope well around your wrist, right?"
"Right, right," Po waved back.
He tightened the noose. Jenny's reaction was immediate. She reared back, bellowed and began running. Po had the rope well secured around his wrist and tried to hold her back. Needless to say an impossible task. He was running after Jenny shouting all sorts of intelligent commands like, "Whoa girl" and "Good girl Jenny" and "Stop ya whore" in fact anything he could think of. Jenny however was in no mood for stopping and if anything gained speed. Po just could not keep up and eventually lost his footing. Jenny kept on running, dragging the screaming Po behind. Red was watching the episode with great amusement. Shouting helpful hints to Po like, "Hold on Po, don't let her go, sure ya have her now." Then stopping to laugh. "You can do it Po, she's slowin' down now, you're wearin' her out."

Eventually Po got the rope free from his wrist and let Jenny go. He stood up slowly and looked down at himself. From his shoes to his head he was covered with cowpat, grass stains and some other stuff that he could not identify. He walked slowly toward Red. He was about thirty feet away and in the time it took to get to the barn Red estimated that Po used every swear word ever spoken and some he had never heard before.

"Friggin' whore of a bastard," mumbled Po as he arrived in front of Red, who held his nose and made a face.

"Jasus Po, ya smell somethin' awful."

"Thanks for tellin' me ya bastard, I wouldn't have noticed."

"Ach now Po, don't be like that, sure it's very funny so it is."

"Funny? What the hell's funny about it?"

"Well sure when ya were tellin' the girls how I fell in the cow shit ya thought it was very funny, didn't ya?"

Po just glared.

"De ya know what Po? There were a couple of wee things I forgot ta tell ya," said Red looking at the sky and rubbing his chin.

"What?" mumbled Po.

"Well firstly, ya know, Jenny hates ropes."

"Ya don't say."

"Secondly, Jenny is one smart cow so she is."

"Smart?"

"Very, wait till ya see this."

Red walked a little way into the field and began tapping the bucket again. Jenny was now back at the far end of the field eating her grass.

"Here Jenny, come on girl, come on Jenny."

Jenny lifted her head, looked and immediately began walking towards Red. When she got to within a few feet of Red he moved forward and patted her head, ushering her into the barn.

"Ya dirty rotten bastard whorin' frigger," Po spat out.

"Now, now Po, temper, temper. Ya see, wee Jenny here is very particular. She won't come in with the other cows ya see, needs to be called specially, a real snob she is for sure."

"Shithead, fruit, wanker."

Red looked Po up and down and shook his head.

"And you're callin' me shithead? What's all that stuff drippin' off ya then?"

Later that night Red was relating the story to Anto and the rest of the gang in Uncle Luigi's when Po arrived all cleaned up and changed.
"Well will ya look who it isn't," smiled Anto. "Howdy partner."
"Frig off you," was Po's only reply.
"A hear ya've taken ta the Cowboy life Po?"
"Frig off."
"And a hear ya have got a likin' for cow shit too."
"Frig off."
"Now Anto, don't be givin' our wee small person a hard time. Sure, he had a grand time slidin' across the grass and the piss and shit up there at the nuns."
"Ya know you're right, he has invented a brand new sport so he has ya know."
"What's that?" asked Red trying to keep a straight face.
"Why, Cowpat Ski'n'," said Anto with some conviction.
"Jasus he's right Po. It could become an Olympic sport. Ya could make a fortune so ya could. Have ya nothing ta say?"
"Frig off."

End

A Nun's Attributes

1960

Red was taking a shortcut through St. Clare's Primary School to the Abbey football ground when he heard his name being called. Looking around he saw Sister Liancha waving at him and went to meet her.
"Hi Sister."
"Hello Red, how are you?"
"Good, good."
"Red, you are just the man I am looking for. Would you be kind enough to give me a hand with something?"
"Sure, no problem."
"I hope I'm not holding you up?"
"No, I'm not in any hurry."
Red followed her into one of the portacabin classrooms.
"Now, I need this cupboard moved to the opposite corner of the room. Would you be able to do that?"
Red opened the door to make sure it was empty, and tried it for weight.
"No, problem. Can I suggest I go and get a wheelbarrow? Ya see if I drag it, it'll mark the floor."
"Whatever you think best," smiled Sister Liancha.

Red went to one of his neighbours he knew had a wheelbarrow, borrowed it, and returned to Sister Liancha. He got the lip of the barrow under the cupboard and had no problem moving it to where it was required to go.
"That's just great, I would never have been able to move that on my own."
"No problem, you're changing the classroom around to face the other way then?"
"Yes, that's exactly what I'm doing. There's more light on the blackboard this way."
"Ah, I understand. Ya have a bit of work ta do yet I see," smiled Red looking around.
"Well, I have all the desks to move and the blackboard."
"Why don't I go and get my mate Po, and we will be glad ta do it for ya?"
"That is very kind of you Red. That would be a great help."

Red arrived at Po's house on North Street and found him outside kicking a football against the wall.
"Po, will ya give me a wee hand ta move some desks for Sister Liancha?"
"Sister 'Headache'?"
"Yep."
"Now?"
"Now."
"Yeah, ok, be with ya in a minute," said Po as he disappeared into the house to collect his coat.

Sister Liancha was known by Red and his friends as Sister 'Headache' because of her enormous breasts. The boys, when they were younger, and in her class, would occasionally get very severe headaches, or fall injuring their heads, which occasioned the Sister to cradle their head into her large breasts, whispering words of sympathy. Headaches were quite popular in that class for some reason.
Red and Po arrived in the classroom and began moving the desks under the directions of Sister Liancha.

"I think a have a bad headache comin' on," whispered Po.
"Shut up you," said Red elbowing Po in the ribs.
"Did ya ever wonder what she'd look like in normal clothes?" asked Po, still whispering.
"Many times," smiled Red.
"So did I. She'd be dead sexy, wouldn't she?"
"Oh yeah, that she would," answered Red looking towards Sister Liancha who was at the other end of the classroom.
"What age do ya think she is?"
"Dunno, maybe 30."
"Would she be that old?"
"Don't be askin' me, I'm hopeless on ages."

The job took just over an hour. All three stood back to admire their work.
"That's just wonderful boys, just wonderful. The classroom even looks bigger."
"Glad ta help," commented Red.
Sister Liancha opened her desk drawer and took out a bag of toffees.
"You can divide these up between you, and thank you very, very much for all your help. It would have taken me the whole weekend to do it on my own."
Red took the sweets from her.
"Thanks Sister, it was no problem. Glad ta help."

After the goodbyes the boys walked the few yards from the classroom onto Castle Street. Both had mouths full of toffee. Po stopped suddenly.
"Jasus."
"What?"
"I've had a brainwave."
"What, what?"
"How big would ya say Sister Liancha's breasts are?"
"Jasus, I dunno, why?"
"Think about it, we could start a book, take bets from all the boys. We'd make a fortune for sure," grinned Po, spinning in a circle.
"Take bets of how big her breasts are?"

"Exactly."
"Are ya out of your tiny mind, ya dick. How could ya possibly measure them?" asked Red.
"Details, details, ya always annoy me with details. I'll come up with somethin'; just need ta think about it."
"You're totally bonkers, crazy, nuts, mad, insane, not to mention out of your skull."
"It'll work I'm tellin' ya. Ok, forget the measuring for a minute, de ya think it would work otherwise, takin' bets and all?"
"Well, I suppose it could work ok," said Red slowly rubbing his chin. "But I could not in anyway see ya measurin' Sister Liancha's chest."
"I'll come up with an idea, have no fear. So, are ya in?"
"Yeah, suppose so," grumbled Red.

The following day Red was feeding the chickens in his back yard when he heard Po's voice.
"Yo shithead."
"And I was havin' such a nice day too."
Po ran the last few yards and jumped on Red's back.
"Get off ya fruit."
"How's my bestest pal in the whole world?"
"No."
"No what?"
"Whatever ya want me ta do, the answer is no."
"Who says I want ya ta do somethin' in the first place?"
"Because I know ya too well."
"Jasus, you're such an auld grump, and sure all I wanted was a wee, small, tiny, little teeny weensy favour that any best friend would do for his best friend that did so many favours for him, like the time he broke his granny's favourite jug and the time…"
"All right, all right. You're worse than an auld one so ya are."
Po made Red sit down on the grass and he explained in detail his plan to measure Sister Liancha's breasts.
"Well?" asked Po.
"Not bad," smiled Red, "Not bad a'tall."

Red and Po worked feverishly the next few days taking bets from everyone they knew on the size of Sister Liancha's chest.
"That Jumpy's a total nutter so he is," laughed Po as he joined Red in the middle snug in Uncle Luigi's.
"What did he do now?" asked Red.
"Guess what he put two bob on?"
"Tell me?"
"Sixty inches," laughed Po.
"Sixty inches, is he mad? Don't answer that, silly question."
"Sixty friggin' inches," laughed Po.
"Well that's two bob in our pocket ta start with anyway," smiled Red sipping his Coke.
"Correct and right, how much have ya got so far?"
Red took a small copybook from his pocket.
"I have, £4.15s so far and a few more ta see. How are ya doin'?"
"Got £5.10s and a few ta see as well."
"Do ya think we should bring Anto in on this?" asked Po.
"As a partner?"
"Yeah."
"Not a bad idea a'tall. He has loads of contacts so he has and could bring in a lot a bets."
"Ok, agreed then, we'll ask him later."

Just then Anto arrived at the snug as if on cue with two coffees. He slid in beside Red.
"Thought yis might like a wee coffee boys," he smiled.
Po and Red exchanged glances.
"Ok Falsoni, what are ya after?"
"Me?" smiled Anto pointing to himself.
"You," answered Red and Po in unison.
"Well a was just thinkin', ya know I have a lot of guys in Dromalane and Church Street not ta mention Chinatown that you boys don't know, right?"
"So?" asked Po.
"Well, this Sister Liancha book yis are runnin'. Now I could bring in a fair bit ta help on that."
"In what way?" asked Po.

"I'm sure I could put in maybe £10 in bets."
"£10 huh? What do ya think Red?"
"Not sure a'tall, this is a real big one we're on Anto, we might lose out by bringing in a third partner."
"But Red, Anto could bring in a lot a bets. I think we should consider it so a do."
"Hmm, I know what ya mean, tell ya what Anto, the deal is goin' down on Monday right? This is Friday, we want free coffee and chips till then and you're in," said Red seriously.
Anto shook hands with Red.
"Deal."
After shaking hands with Po he asked, "Now, the big question is, how are ya goin' ta measure her chest?"
"Ah, now that is the big secret. We can't just go around tellin' everyone or someone else might try it."
"Good point, but, the guys I take money off in bets will want ta know how it will be proven?"
"Tell them not ta worry. There will be three independent witnesses there to verify the result."
"Ok, sounds good, tell me then, how are ya goin' ta do it?"
"Ya have no chance Anto," laughed Red.

Monday afternoon arrived and Po called for Red at 4pm.
"Right, are ya ready?" asked Po.
"You've got the basketball I see," said Red pointing at the ball under Po's arm.
"And the tape goes over the ball, is that right?"
"I'll explain on the way, come on will ya."
"Who did ya get for witnesses?"
"Jammy, Kitter an Blackie, they are already over in the convent field."
"Ok, so let's go then."
The two boys met up with the rest at the convent field.
"Are yis ready ta go?"
"Yeah, but where will Sister Liancha be now?" asked Jammy.
"In her classroom. She is always there up to about 4.30pm."
All five headed in the direction of Sister Liancha's classroom. Red peeped through the window and stepped back.

"Ok, she's there, marking books at her desk."
"Ok, let's go. Now ya have a very important job in this whole thing Red, ya sure ya know what ta do?"
"I do, I do, stop naggin'. The question is, will she go for it?"
"She will, don't worry."

"Hello Sister," said Po entering the classroom.
"Well hello," said Sister Liancha looking up from her books.
"Sister, we were all wonderin' if ya would be kind enough ta do us a wee favour?"
"If I can, I would be delighted to, what is it?"
"Well it's like this. We were playin' basketball with some of the girls from Castle Street. We had an argument about the length of their arms. I was saying that their arms were the same length as an adult woman's arms. They said no way. We were wonderin' if ya would be kind enough ta help us prove it?"
"What do you want me do?" smiled Sister Liancha standing up.
"We would like ya to hold this basketball at full stretch out in front of ya and we will measure the distance all the way around, then we will do the same with one of the girls and we will see who is right."
"Well that doesn't sound too difficult. I would be delighted to make peace between Castle Street's male and female basketball players," smiled Sister Liancha.
Po instructed her how to hold the ball out in front of her chest with her arms outstretched. He then took one end of a measuring tape he produced from his pocket and handed the other end to Red. He went behind her and pressed the end of the tape into her back. Red took his end and ran the tape along her arm, across her hands and the ball in between, and along the other arm to meet Po at Sister Liancha's back. The three witnesses went behind to verify the measurement. When Red handed Po his end of the tape, Po instructed him loudly to go to the front and make sure the tape was exactly in the middle of the ball between Sister Liancha's hands. Red did so. He pulled the tape out a little to get his finger underneath.
"Is that straight Po?" he asked.
"Let me tighten it a bit," Po answered.

Red moved his finger downwards and looked up. Po was looking around Sister Liancha's shoulder. He winked and pulled the tape tight. Red's finger and the tape, at the same time, slid downward and was pulled into Sister Liancha's chest. Red felt his finger right between her breasts.

"Sorry Sister, Po what are ya doing back there?" snarled Red stepping back.

"Sorry, sorry, do it again. I pulled too tight."

Red placed the tape once again at the front, across the middle of the basketball.

"I make that exactly seven feet," said Po.

The tape was removed from the smiling Sister Liancha.

"Glad I could help."

"Ya'll never know how valuable you were to us Sister," smiled Po.

After the goodbyes, the boys left Sister Liancha to get on with her work.

"Well?" asked Red impatiently.

"Well what?" asked Po.

"You are askin' for it Hillen."

"Oh, the measurement ya mean?"

"The friggin' measurement, now," snarled Red.

"Let's see, ah, exactly seven feet," said Po checking his notes.

"That's it, you're goin' ta feel serious pain Hillen."

"Why didn't ya say, it's her chest measurement ya wanted."

Red made a grab for Po.

"All right, all right, let me look will ya?"

Po fumbled through his notebook.

"Let's see, I made it 42 inches."

"Boys," came the voice of Sister Liancha.

They all stopped and looked back. Sister Liancha was leaning out of the classroom window.

"Are you passing Mrs. Daly's house?"

"Yeah, we are Sister."

"Great, would you be kind enough to deliver something to her please?"

Red and Po walked back to the window.
"No problem Sister," smiled Red.
Sister Liancha reached down inside the top of her habit and slowly pulled out a black cotton veil folded a number of times.
"I had nowhere else to keep this folded, almost forgot about it," she smiled. "Give this to Mrs. Daly, she's expecting it."
"Ok Sister, bye," smiled Red taking her veil.

When they were about 20 yards from the classroom Po was the first to speak.
"Damn, shit, bastard, whore, frig and frig again."
"What?" asked Red.
"That means the whole friggin' thing was for nothin'. The measurements are no friggin' good now."
"Suppose ya'r right."
"So then are all bets off?" asked Jammy.
"Looks that way," replied Red. "The veil she had under her habit will totally throw the measurements out for sure."
"Yeah, guess so."
After a few minutes of walking in silence, Po grabbed Red's arm.
"I have an idea."
"No."
"I have it from good authority that Johnny Murtagh's willie is over eight inches long."
"No."
"But it would be easy to verify."
"No."
"Think of the money we could take on bets, would make up for today."
"No."
"But it would be a brilliant idea."
"No."
"Ah, come on Red."
"No."
"Please?"
"No."

"Pretty please?"
"No."
"Can ya not think of anythin' else ta say except no?"
"No."
"Shit."
"No."

End

The Dog Race

1960

"Well," mumbled Po as he caught up with his mate Red. "Where ya headin'?"
"Goin' ta get snuff for ma granny."
"How do they take that stuff? I tried it once an a sneezed for half an hour."
"They get used ta it I suppose, sure look at us when we started smokin' for the first time. My friggin' head was spinnin' and I couldn't stop coughin'."
"Yeah, true, remember that all right."
"So what's the story with Anto, I heard he was in a fight?" Red asked.
"Well, don't know all the details, but some supposed hard man from Bessbrook got a bit cheeky in the café. He made some remarks about Uncle Luigi. Anto asked him to leave. From what I hear he refused and Anto sort of helped him…" Po laughed, "…his head hit every snug on the way out and then outside he took a swing at Anto…big mistake."
"So what happened ta him?"
"He spent the night getting stitched up in Daisy Hill Hospital."
"Sounds about right, stupid bastard."
"Are you entering Snowball in the dog race?"

"Don't know…might."
"I'm goin' to enter our Rascal this year."
"What? Are ya out of your tiny mind?"
"Rascal's a fast runner so he is."
"I'm sure he is, but sure his legs are only six inches long. He couldn't keep up with big dogs."
"Ah, ya didn't hear did ya? They've changed the rules this year. There's four different categories…small…medium…large and greyhounds."
"Who told ya that?"
"Billy Crummie."
"Well if that's true I agree with it for sure, gives everyone a chance. So that's actually four categories plus the one you'll be enterin' Rascal in."
"What are ya talkin' about, the one I'm enterin' Rascal in?"
"Well, sure that would be the 'Rat Category', wouldn't it?"
Red was anticipating Po's swing and was able to dodge it.
"Bastard."
"Now Po, don't be like that. It's nice that you've taken in a rat…most people don't like them."
Red wasn't quick enough the second time and Po's fist caught him in the chest.

****

The great day had arrived and the Abbey Sports Field was packed with dogs and their owners.
Red was talking to some of the other dog owners when he saw Po coming with Rascal on a lead.
Po motioned him to move away with him out of the hearing of the group.
"What?" asked Red.
"Now listen carefully will ya? I want ya ta walk along with me and just act as if we are in conversation, right?"
"What are ya up ta?"
"A have a plan."
"Haven't ya always?"
"It's a good one, if it works," Po smiled and patted his coat pocket.

"What have ya got?"
"Minced beef."
"What for?"
"Ah, now that's the good bit ya see. Our Rascal loves mince so he does but he hates peppermint."
"So?"
"Well, I mixed loads of peppermint through the mince so a have. The other dogs will go for it but our Rascal will just ignore it so he will."
"I think I see, so what are ya goin' ta do?"
"Walk with me will ya? Now I cut a hole in ma pocket and I'm goin' ta drop the meat all the way across the course. The other dogs in the race will go for it but Rascal won't, ya see?"
Red just shook his head.
"What? De ya think it won't work?"
"No, it's not that, I never stop being amazed at the way your wee evil mind works."

Po and Red walked diagonally across the grass track just before the Small Dog's Race. Po dropped all his minced beef as planned and they returned to the starting area where the other owners were gathering. They were quite a mixed bunch including mums, dads, grannies, sisters, friends and of course the dogs themselves. The way the races were organised was that a friend or relative would hold the dog. The owner would go to the far end of the field and on the command of the Official Starter, call their dogs, who would then be released.

The starter raised his flag and convinced that all was ready, with great aplomb lowered the flag and shouted 'Go'. The dogs, all with eyes fixed on their calling owners took off with great excitement and speed. Halfway along the track however, a couple of the dogs stopped and seemed to be sniffing the ground. Then more stopped and still more until the only dog still racing was Rascal Hillen. At the end of the allotted race track Rascal arrived and jumped into the waiting arms of his owner, Po. Since the dogs had eaten up all the 'evidence' there was nothing the owners could complain about to the officials even though they tried.

A proud Po was handed the Small Dog's Category Cup at the end of the day to great cheers and applause from his friends and family. Red too was a happy dog owner as his dog Snowball won the Medium Dog's Category.

A celebratory fish and chip supper was being consumed later that day in Uncle Luigi's.
"Well what de ya think?" Po asked Red.
"Sure you're nothin' short of a wee genius."
"Frig me, ya always understate everything so ya do."
"So did ya say anythin' ta the other owners, a saw ya talkin' ta them?"
"Naw, just hard luck shit and that, but de ya know what a wanted ta say?"
"What?"
"He who eats and runs away, lives ta run another day."
"Devious wee frigger."

End

The Ice Lolly Swindle

1960

"Two penny ice lollies please," said Red to Sheila Bradley, who was standing behind the sweet counter at Bradley's Grocery shop.
"I'll get them Sheila," came the voice of Po who was standing behind Red in the shop.
Po went around the opposite counter to where the ice cream was kept in the cabinet freezer. He opened it and after shuffling some boxes around, took out two lollies, showed them to Sheila and returned to the middle of the shop. Red gave Sheila one shilling and while waiting for his change noticed Po looking at the goods behind the third counter in the shop. When the transaction was completed and the two were outside Red turned to Po.
"What were ya lookin' at behind the counter?"
"Them little shoe brushes on the top shelf. How much are they, de ya know?"
"Tuppence I think, why?"
"Hmmm."
"Why?"
"Just thinkin' about something. Ya know the little slips of paper they put in the penny lollies? If ya get one ya get a free lolly?"

"Yeah."
"Well if ya lift the paper of the lolly a little ya can see if there's a slip inside…see?"
Po produced a slip of greaseproof paper from his pocket.
"Ya got a freebee," smiled Red.
"Yep, and I think I might have found a way ta get a lot more too."
"Tell me."
"It's the wee brushes on the top shelf. If we ask for a lolly and one of them wee brushes, Sheila will have to go and get the steps, climb up ta get one, come back down, sit it on the counter, put the steps away and return to the other counter, she'll have her back to the ice cream counter all the time ya see. This will give me loads a time at the freezer."
"So?"
"So, stupid, while she's doing all that, I can be lookin' through the lollies for the free slips. I think I could get a load of them ya know and all it would cost would be the tuppence for the brush."
"What a smart little person ya are," laughed Red.
"Piss off."
"I'll bet your dog must be very proud of ya."
"We will try it on Saturday when we are goin' ta the mornin' show in the Frontier."
"Sounds like an idea ta me," said Red.
"Now one other thing, when I go ta the freezer, ya have ta shout ta me and tell me ta get ya a red one."
"Why?"
"That way ya see, Sheila won't be alerted if I am a long time at the freezer. I'll be lookin' for a red one."
"Smart," laughed Red.

Saturday morning arrived and Red and Po entered Bradley's shop to put Po's idea into action. Everything went according to plan. Red asked for the small shoe brush and a red lolly. Sheila went and got the stepladder, Po offered as usual to get the lolly.
"Po, don't forget I want a red one," shouted Red to Po making sure Sheila heard.
"Yeah, yeah, I heard ya the first time," answered Po.

A few minutes later they were out of the shop and running down Castle Street. They both stopped at the top of Hyde Market.
"Well?"
"A can't move ma friggin' hands," complained Po.
"Why's that?"
"They're frozen friggin' stiff so they are."
"For God's sake a thought ya were goin' ta say ya had been paralyzed by God as a punishment for stealin' Bradley's lollies."
"Hold on a minute you. I didn't steal anythin'. The slips they put in are for free lollies so how could a be stealin' something that's free?"
"Good point. Ah sure you're just a great wee honest person so ya are."
"Smart arse."
"Well how many did ya get anyway?"
"I got four. I noticed on the box it said there were ten free lollies in every box and the box was half empty so I suppose there were some already gone," said Po.
"Four? Jasus," exclaimed Red. "We'll go back in a few minutes an get two freebees for the Pictures."
"Naw, leave it till tomorra, just ta be safe."
"Ok."
"What I like about it is that she'll not miss anythin', will she?"
"True and sure she won't be out of pocket either will she?"
"No, you're right."
"I don't think I've come across this before," mused Red.
"Come across what?"
"Honest thieving."
"Correct and right, sure we're true saints so we are."

End

The Teacher Affair

1960

"So, he said I had ta go with him ta Warrenpoint in the van. He was deliverin' wood to Kelly's," said Po.
"But what had it ta do with him?" asked Red.
"Jasus, are ya listenin' ta me or not? A told ya already."
"So tell me again will ya? You're worse than an auld one."
"Right, now listen this time will ya? Mom was cleanin' ma room, right? She found the yokes in the drawer and…"
"The condoms, right?"
"Right, the French Letters, the Rubbers, the Condoms, will ya pay attention will ya? She went and got ma Uncle John to have a talk with me ta see what I was up ta. She would have normally went ta ma da, but he's in England for the next two weeks, right?"
"With ya now, go on."
"Well, we were in the van for about ten minutes when he says… 'So, I understand ya might be havin' sex young fella'. Well, Jasus, I nearly shit. I didn't know what the hell he was on about."
"So what did ya say?"
"I just kept ma face straight and a says…'Why do ya say that Uncle John?' Well, sure he went on ta tell me then how mom found the yokes in ma room."

"Jasus, so what did ya say?" asked Red.
"I had ta do some fast thinkin' so I did, so I says…'well, I'm sort of havin' an affair'."
"Havin' an affair?" said Red with some exaggeration.
"What did ya want me ta say?"
"Jasus, ya could have told the truth and said that ya had them in case ya met a blind girl who wasn't too fussy."
"Oh, sure aren't ya a real card aren't ya?"
"So who did ya say ya were havin' the affair with then?"
"First of all I said I would tell him if it was strictly between the two of us, he agreed."
"And…?"
"Sure a had ta make somethin' up didn't I?"
"So…?"
"I said, Miss O'Hagan."
Red's mouth dropped open in genuine astonishment.
"You're takin' the piss?"
"No."
"Miss O'Hagan the music teacher?"
"Yeah."
"Ya told your uncle ya were havin' an affair with Miss O'Hagan?"
"Yeah."
"Ya did in your arse."
"I did, honest ta God."
"No way, a know you're stupid, but you're not that stupid."
"It just came out."
"Frig off."
"I did I'm tellin' ya, a got a bit flustered and just said the first thing that came into ma head."
"What did John say?"
"He was quiet for a minute and then he says, 'Jasus, a school teacher? What age is she?' I told him she was about thirty. He says, 'Frig me, we'd better not tell your mom that, she'd freak out altogether'."
"He was right, that's for sure."
"Then he says, 'What's this Miss O'Hagan like?' I described her ta him and ya know what he said?"
"What?"

"He said, 'Jasus, friggin' schools have sure changed so they have. You get friggin' Marilyn Monroe, when I was at school a got Mother Mary hatchet face'."
The two broke into laughter.
"So what are ya goin' ta say ta your mom?"
"Oh, I already agreed with Uncle John what ta say, I'll tell her I was holdin' them for you."
"Ya better not, Jasus, and what if she tells my ma?"
"Naw, she won't. I'll tell her ya just found them."
"Sure, anytime ya get in trouble, just blame me."
"Well, sure ya know…Miss O'Hagan fancies me anyway."
"Ya need to see a doctor, de ya know that, better still, why don't ya go an boil your head?"
"She does, a can tell."
"You're outta your tree, Miss O'Hagan fancies you?"
"It's the way she looks at me, ya know, with longin', desire."
"Jasus help me, Po would ya ever get a grip of your knickers before someone hears ya sayin' that, ya'll get yourself locked up in a padded cell."
"You're just jealous Morgan cause you're not as handsome as me."
"Oh God."
"What can I say? When ya got it, ya got it."
"Ya live in cloud cuckoo land Po."
"Ya know, I might just have an idea formin' here," smiled Po looking at the sky.
"I don't want ta hear," said Red seriously.
"Well look at it this way, if it was thought that I was havin' an affair with herself, sure wouldn't I have a name and a half in the town. All the women would be dyin' ta get out with me. They would think I was a right stud."
"Yeah, and when your mom found out you'd look like ya just did ten rounds with Joe Lewis."
"Thought of that, a would be very discreet ya see, I wouldn't admit or deny anything, play it cool like."
"Do what ya like, but keep me outta the whole thing, I think ya'r a boot short of a football kit."

A few days later Red was walking along Hill Street when he heard his name being called.
"Red…Red…hold up…," came the high pitched voice of Jumpy. With him was the Bishop. Red stopped to wait on them.
Jumpy's voice dropped to a whisper as he reached Red.
"Is it true?"
"Is what true?" whispered Red mocking Jumpy.
"About Po and Miss whats-her-face?"
"What about them?"
"Ah come on Red, ya know the inside story for sure," put in the Bishop.
"Haven't a clue what ya are all talkin' about."
"Po and Miss O'Hagan, ya know, havin' an affair."
"Who told ya that then?"
"Everybody's talkin' about it, but Po won't say a word."
"Well, I can't say that he is and I can't say that he isn't, that's for sure," smiled Red.
"You're holdin' back Red, ya know, don't ya?"
"All I know is that I need a half crown for the weekend and I can't figure out where am goin' ta get it."
"He's useless, come on and we'll ask Anto," said Jumpy to Bishop, who nodded. They both raced off towards Uncle Luigi's.

****

"Come here ya wee rat," said Red through gritted teeth when he met Po that evening.
"Hiya carrot head," smiled Po.
"Ya did it, didn't ya?"
"Did what?" asked Po innocently.
"Ya had ta go and start the rumour didn't ya?"
"Well, I just sorta dropped a hint and it was jumped on," smiled Po wistfully.
"Jumped on? The whole friggin' town's talkin' about it."
"Didn't a tell ya that? I knew it would be big."
"You're gonna get yourself in big shit, take my word," Red said seriously.

"Not a'tall. Ya see, I never really said anythin' ya see. I sort of hinted and let them make up the story themselves. I never actually said I was havin' an affair. I looked it up in the dictionary, it's called, innuendo, great word, isn't it?"
"You're still walkin' on thin ice so ya are."
"No way, sure they're all lookin' at me now as if I was a great lover or somethin'."

The two went into Uncle Luigi's where they were greeted by Anto who came around from behind the counter to meet them.
"Sit down here," he said pointing to an empty snug.
"Well?"
"Well what?" said Po innocently.
"What are ya up to Hillen?"
"Me, now why would ya think I was up ta somethin'?"
"Red, what's goin' on?" Anto gave up on Po and tried his luck with Red.
"I told him he's not the full shillin' but sure when did he ever listen ta me?"
"Is there any truth ta it?"
"Jasus Anto, I'm surprised ya even asked that?"
"I friggin' knew it, what are ya up ta ya wee bugger?"
"I can't help what people believe can I?"
"But you're lettin' them believe it aren't ya?"
"Maybe."
"Maybe my arse. Now come on, what are ya up ta?"
"He thinks it will raise his profile ya see Anto. All the girls in the town will think he's a stud ya see and will be lookin' ta get out with him," put in Red.
"Jasus," puffed Anto.
"Well, it's workin' so far. Your one Mary McCullough and Joan Hennessey were all smiles and hello's ta me this mornin'. They would never have noticed me before."
Anto looked at Red.
"He might be right ya know."
"Jasus Christ Anto, don't you start backin' him up for God's sake. He's bad enough as it is."

"But the idea is sound isn't it. All the women will think he's a stud and be fightin' with each other ta get out with him."
"I'm goin' home," said Red in a depressed voice.
"No, I'm serious. There could be somethin' in this ya know."
"What the hell are ya on about Anto?"
"Well, think about it. Your one McCullough, or as she is better known, 'Ice Knickers'. Just think of the book I could run on Po gettin' out with her on a date?"
Red sat back and looked up at the ceiling. He had to admit to himself that the idea was not at all bad.
"Well?" asked Anto.
"Maybe, but it would have ta be handled right."
"It will be."
"Hi yous. I'm here too ya know. What do I get out of it?" put in Po.
"Don't worry about that Po, you'll get your cut, don't worry," answered Anto quickly.

From that moment on, voices in the snug were lowered to a whisper and the conspiracy was born. Anto was to set up the betting on Po getting a date with Mary 'Ice Knickers' McCullough. Red's job was to spread the rumour saying to everyone that he had taken a bet with Anto that Po would not have a chance with her.

By the end of that weekend, Anto had taken more than twenty bets. Part two of the plan depended on Red talking to Mary McCullough. They knew that she worked in her father's shop on Canal Street. On Monday night at around six o'clock, Red, by total coincidence, bumped into her leaving the shop.
"Hello Mary."
"Hi Red, where are you headin'?"
"Into town, you?"
"Me too, goin' ta meet Joan at the Flo."
"So, how are things with yourself?"
"Good, and you?"
"Good, ya know I was just talkin' about you this mornin'."
"Ya were, who to?"
"Po Hillen."

"What were ya talkin' about me for?"
"Well it wasn't so much me as Po. He was goin' on about ya non stop."
"What was he sayin'?"
"Ah for God's sake, I'd better not tell ya, only give ya a big head," laughed Red.
"Tell me, tell me," pleaded Mary.
Red looked at her. He had to admit she was a bit special. She had large blue eyes that lit up when she smiled. She had quite a nice figure too and from the way she walked Red suspected she knew it.
"Well, he was sayin' how beautiful ya are. How ya remind him of some film star or other that he's mad about, how ya would never go out with him in a million years because…sure it doesn't matter."
"It does matter, what did he say?"
"I'm not sure I should be tellin' ya this ya know. It was sort of, in confidence."
"I won't tell a soul, I swear ta God."
"Well he was sayin' this, not me. He was sayin' that ya were a terrible snob, that ya thought you were too good for the likes of him."
"Po said that?"
"Yep."
"Sure that's not true Red, ya know that."
"Well ta tell ya the truth Mary, there are a few of the lads that think that way."
"Oh my God, a mean, why would they think that?"
"Well, have ya ever been out with any of the lads that hang about Uncle Luigi's?"
"No, don't think so."
"There ya go then."
"But I like Po, I think he's a nice guy."
"Do ya, do ya really?" said Red smiling at Mary.
"Of course I do."
"So would ya go out with him then?"
"He never asked me."
"Suppose he did, would ya? It would stop people saying ya were a snob if nothin' else, wouldn't it?"

"I would go out with Po if he asked me."
"Well sure, leave it with me and I will have a chat with himself and set it up."

So that was that. Game, set and match. Po got out on a date with Mary 'Ice Knickers' McCullough and got ten shillings from Anto for his trouble. Red too got ten shillings and it was estimated by Red that Anto made over ten pounds on the whole affair.

****

Red and Po were walking along Boat Street with their football gear slung over their shoulders on their way to play at the back of Newry's Showground.
"Ya know, I was givin' the matter a lot of thought, a have ta bring it ta a close," said Po seriously.
"What are ya talkin' about?"
"I know it will hurt her feelin's, but it's for the best all round."
"What, what?"
"It's the age thing, and of course the time thing," went on Po unconcerned at Red's impatience.
"Po, you are gettin' close ta a kick up the arse."
"It's this Miss O'Hagan thing. I am goin' ta have ta drop her now ya know, it's just not fair on her. My time these days is just not my own. I know ya wouldn't have any experience in this field Red, but when ya'r as popular as me with the ladies it can be very time consumin' and not to mention, stressful."

Po reached the football ground safely without Red being able to catch him.

End

The Set Up

1960

Po had arrived at Red's house on Castle Street to tell him about a very serious incident that happened the night before. A gang from the other side of the town, the St. John Martin Gardens area, known locally as 'Chinatown', stopped Topcoat Anderson on his way home, and gave him a beating.
"So what happened?" asked Red seriously.
"From what a was told they all jumped him and gave him a hidin'. He ended up with stitches in his face and his whole body all bruised as far as a know," answered Po.
"The cowardly bastards. Typical of them so it is. They wouldn't pick a fight if it was one ta one."
"That's what I was sayin' ta Anto this mornin'."
"Well, they'll not get away with it I can tell ya."
"No, hold on a minute Red. There's more than one way ta skin a rabbit ya know."
"What de ya mean?"
"Well if we get the lads together and go lookin' for them and give them a hidin' back, sure it will only start a whole war between us and Chinatown."

"So what?"
"Let me come up with a plan first, right? I think I might know a way ta get the bastards back so they won't know what hit them."
"It better be a good one Po."
"Don't worry, it will be," Po promised seriously.

****

The gang had all gathered at Uncle Luigi's. They were out the back of the shop sitting on bags of potatoes.
"Well Po, come on, tell us, what have ya come up with?" asked Anto.
"They all go ta the Bucket for the Record Hop at the weekends, right?"
"Yeah."
"That's where we'll get them. Anto, can ya get me some of them big drums the oil comes in?"
"I suppose so, why do ya want them?"
"An can ya fill them with the old used oil?"
"Yeah, Uncle Luigi would be glad ta get rid of it so he would."
"Right, now listen up, this is what we are goin' ta do."

****

Saturday night arrived and Po's plan was well into its first stage. Jumpy Jones was standing at the entrance door to the Bucket at the top of the thirty steps leading to it. The rest of the gang sneaked the four drums of 'used chipper' oil up the back stairs. Red had managed to borrow the key to the Bucket's flat roof. Anto, Red, Po and Topcoat were now on the roof waiting.

The Chinatown crowd arrived as expected. There were eight of them in all. They climbed the steps to the front door laughing and joking with each other as they went. Just before they reached the door, Jumpy closed it and barred it on the inside. On the command of Po, the four masked men on the roof tilted the drums of oil over the small wall that went all the way around, followed immediately with paper bags of flour. The scene below was pure pandemonium. The oil hit its target perfectly as did the flour right on top of the Chinatown gang. They were all looking like snowmen at this stage. Many swear words graced the air that night but not from the masked boys on the roof who were to say the least, having a good time. The Chinatown mob left quickly to the jeers and laughter of the crowds now arriving, running as fast as they could down Hyde Market. But they found to their dismay that running was not all that easy with their feet covered in oil.

Later that night the boys all met up in Uncle Luigi's for Coke and chips.
"Worked a treat," laughed Anto.
"Did we get all that oil hosed away, I don't want ta get barred outta the Bucket?" asked Po.
"All gone. What was left we covered with sawdust. We'll clear that tomorrow. We told Benny the caretaker what we did and he was all for it, couldn't stop laughin' so he couldn't," beamed Topcoat. "The Chinatown crowd took most of it with them anyway. It was almost worth gettin' a beatin' for."
The whole gang was now engulfed in laughter.
"Po, your wee plan was great, ya were right, much better than a war for sure, and better still, they didn't know who it was either," laughed Red.
"Correct and right, the 'Greasy Snowmen' from Chinatown will more than likely stay in their own part of the town in future," finished Po.

The Boat Race

1960

It was a quiet time of the day at Uncle Luigi's. Anto was sitting in the first snug chatting with Red, Po, Jumpy and Topcoat.

"When did ya come up with this one?" asked Red who was sitting across from Anto.

"Last night, ya have ta admit its brilliant…isn't it?"

"Well, it does tickle the fancy for sure, but will ya get enough entrants?"

"Are ya serious? Before the day is out I will have twenty at least."

"I think it's a great idea Anto…but what's the catch?"

"No catch, our boat wins, I take all the bets, we'll make a fortune," laughed Anto leaning back.

"Now hold on a minute, our boat wins? How do ya figure that?"

"Well sure we just have ta have the best boat in the race, that's all."

"And how do we do that?" asked Topcoat.

"This is where Red comes in, now Red, would your Uncle Pajoe help with the buildin' of the boat?"

"I suppose he would, but sure that doesn't mean it would be the best in the race does it?"

"Isn't he one of the best carpenters in the town isn't he?" went on Anto.
"At makin' tables and chest a'drawers, not boats."
"Same friggin' difference."
"We would have ta have an angle," put in Po.
"Right, that we would, that's where you come in," continued Anto. "You're the devious wee bastard, the planner, the one who comes up with all the ideas, so that end of it is down ta you."
"Friggin' great."
"Well?" said Anto looking around the faces in the snug. "Is it a go, Red?"
"Well, sure we'll have a go."
"Po?"
"Ok."
"Topcoat?"
"Why not."
"Jumpy?"
"I'm all for it."
"Right let's go for it then," smiled Anto.
"Wow, hold on a minute Anto. Who's goin' ta be in the boat?" asked Red.
"You and Po," answered Anto.
"Oh, I see, you get the idea, make the money and I get ta do the dirty work."
"Now don't be like that Red, sure you're the fittest and the wee ugly one is the most devious. The perfect pair," laughed Anto.
Everyone agreed and Red was shouted down when he started to complain.

The rules of the race were simple. All the boats had to be home made and be able to carry two people. Even the oars had to be home made. There would be a prize for the most original design. Red told his Uncle Pajoe about the idea and he loved it. He was excited about the whole concept of building a boat and set about the planning immediately.

A few days later Red heard voices coming from Pajoe's work shed and went to investigate. He found Po and Pajoe deep in conversation over a pile of sketches and scribbled plans.

"How's it goin'?" asked Red.
"We have the basic plan, well at least I had, until he arrived and demanded a major change."
"What's he want now?"
"A hole in the floor of the boat. He wants the centre to be open like a catamaran."
"What on earth for?"
"Don't ask me, he was just about to explain his great plan."
"Ok, so tell us, why does it have ta be open in the middle?" Red asked Po.
"Never mind that now but it's very important to the whole design."
"If ya say so."

Three days later, the boat was finished and the whole gang had gathered in Red's back garden to see it.
"She looks grand Po. Will she float?" asked Jumpy.
"No, it's a submarine."
"Why is it open in the middle?" asked Topcoat.
"I'll show you that later."
"It's not very big," said Anto.
"Well the smaller it is the faster it is," answered Po.
"Will two people fit in it?" asked Red.
"Since you will be one of them ya better try it," said Po, "and take your shoes off and tread very lightly."
Red did as he was told and slowly got into the boat. It was in fact quite close to being a catamaran. There were two bows, linked together. The same at the back, with a single seating bench across the width of the boat just a couple of feet back from the centre.
"Well, get in," Red said to Po.
"No, I'm not goin' ta be in the boat ya see."
"You're not?"
"No, Jumpy will do it."
"So where will you be?"
Po smiled and motioned everyone closer.
"Listen carefully," he whispered.
"What's all this about?" whispered Red copying Po's hushed tones.

"This is why I'm not goin' ya see," said Po tilting the boat onto its side, and pointing to two handles, fixed underneath, one on either side of the hole. "These are for my hands ya see, right? The hole there in the centre will be for my snorkel. I will be under the boat wearing our Jim's flippers. Are ya gettin' it yet?"
"Jasus Po, you're goin to be pushin' the boat from underneath," gasped Red.
"That's brilliant Po, your best idea yet," piped in Topcoat.
"Ya see with the flippers I'll be able ta push the boat faster and no one will know I'm there. I'll slip into the canal further down and swim underwater until I am under the boat. Then I'll stick the snorkel up through the middle of the boat. De ya see there?" said Po pointing to a bulldog clip on the back of the bench. "I clip the snorkel into that and we're ready ta go."
"Jasus Po, this is very complicated so it is. Will it work?"
"Don't worry about that, I'll make it work."
"Ya better."
"What are we goin' ta call her?" asked Anto.
"Have already thought of that," laughed Po. "I named her 'The Snorkel'."

****

The day of the boat race arrived. There were fourteen entries. Everything from empty oil drums strapped together to simple rafts. Po had managed to get himself under the boat without anyone noticing. Everything was ready for the starter, Anto, to drop his chequered flag. He did so with great style and the race was on. Red and Jumpy began paddling with the make shift oars as fast as they could. The Snorkel was soon in the lead and moving ahead rapidly. The race was to run between the Savoy Bridge and Ballybot Bridge which was about five hundred yards. The Snorkel was now over five lengths in front. The paddling was tough going but Red and Jumpy were working hard. Soon they were in sight of the finish line. Red heard Jumpy shout.
"Ya whorin' bastard."
Looking over he saw the problem immediately, Jumpy had dropped his oar into the water and the boat was beginning to turn in a circle.

Needless to say, Po, underneath had no idea what was going on and was still swimming away trying to push the boat forward.
"Get the friggin' thing quick Jumpy," yelled Red .
"How the frig am a goin' ta get it?" Jumpy shouted back.
The oar was now about ten feet away.
"Jump in and get it for Christ's sake."
"I can't swim that good."
"Shit," roared Red.
He dropped his oar and jumped into the water, swam the few yards to where the oar was floating and retrieved it. After clambering back into the boat it took a few minutes to get it back on course. By this time there were two other boats coming right up on them. They managed to get going again however and regained a good lead and stayed that way until they crossed the finish line to the great cheers and applause from the gang who had all gathered on the Ballybot Bridge.

Later in Uncle Luigi's there were great celebrations with free fish and chips put up by Anto. Red missed the start of the party as he had to go home and change his clothes. When he arrived he got a round of applause from all there.
"Well we did it," laughed Anto.
"I did it," corrected Po.
"That ya did ma wee genius," said Red putting his arms around Po and givin' him a hug.
"Get off ya fruit," complained Po.

Red, Po and Jumpy got two pounds each from Anto who refused to say how much he made on the day. But his broad grin told everyone it was plenty.
The story of the fastest boat ever built in Castle Street is now legend. The true story of Newry's fastest ever underwater, breathing propeller was kept strictly secret.

End

The Snowman

1960

"Our Pajoe was sayin' he was listenin' to the weather forecast and they were expecting heavy snow tonight," said Red.
"Jasus, I hope so, I love the snow," commented Po.
"Me too," added Ginger.
The boys were on the way home after having a game of football in the little park on the Warrenpoint Road.
"Po where is that sleigh we had last year?" asked Red.
"I think it's in our attic, I'll have a look when a get home."
"I have ta get that bugger Anto back for last year so a have," said Ginger.
"What did he do?" asked Po.
"What did he do? I'll tell ya what he did, he only covered a crack in the ice with snow in the Barge Basin down there at Sands Mill and called me over. Not knowin' about the crack a course, a cut across the corner of the basin and down a went, up ta ma arse in freezin' friggin' water."
Both Po and Red burst out laughing.
"Not funny ya bastards."
"I know, poor Ginger, sure your poor wee willie must have been in an awful state," said Po with a straight face.

"And smaller than usual too, but wait, what am a talkin' about, sure that would be impossible," Red managed to get in between laughs.
"Well, this year a will get ma own back so a will."
"Good for ya Ginger, have ya any ideas? Come ta think of it, a wouldn't mind gettin' that Anto bugger ma own self," smiled Po looking at Red.
"Well, go for it, I'll back ya for sure," said Red.
"We have a mission then. Red you get Bishop, Jumpy and Dunno on board. We'll meet in the Mall bus shelters at seven tonight, right?"

Everyone turned up for the meeting even Topcoat.
"Well?" Red asked Po.
"Well what?"
"Have ya a plan?"
"Not yet."
"Brilliant. What about you guys, any ideas?"
There was total silence until Topcoat spoke up.
"Ya know, it was when yis were talkin' about the snow a remembered a trick played on one of ma neighbours many years ago with a snowman."
"Was it a good one?" asked Bishop.
"If it's done right, it could be very good," grinned Topcoat.
"Well, tell us for Christ's sake," said Red impatiently.
"Let's see now, they had an old manikin ya see..."
"What's a manikin?" asked Jumpy.
"A dummy," answered almost everyone together.
"Just like your own self, only it doesn't smoke," put in Po.
He leaned out of the way of Jumpy's fist.
"They covered the dummy in snow and let it set. They then sprinkled some water on it to make the snow harden as I remember."
"And how did they scare the neighbour with it?" asked Po.
"Ah, that was the clever bit ya see. They organised the neighbour to come and see it, but beforehand they scraped out the back of the snowman, took out the dummy, which left the snowman hollow ya see. One of the lads got inside and when the neighbour arrived he began talkin' ta him," laughed Topcoat.
"Jasus, I like it, I like it so a do," said Po seriously.

"Is it worth a go?" Red asked looking around everyone.
There was general agreement. Po was put in charge of all the arrangements.
"Can a mention a small possible hitch?" said Bishop?
"What?" asked Red.
"Maybe ya haven't noticed yet, but it hasn't snowed?"
Everyone laughed.
"He's right though," said Po. "Assumin' it snows tonight we'll go ahead, if not, we'll just put it on hold until it does, everyone agreed?"
"Agreed," they all said together.

For once the weather forecast was right, three inches of snow fell overnight. The boys all gathered in Red's back yard the next morning and began building the snowman. Po managed to borrow an old manikin from somewhere and the snowman was built around it.

****

"Well, what's happenin'," smiled Anto as he slid into the snug beside Po and Topcoat.
"Some snowfall," commented Po.
"Sure was, have yis anythin' planned?" asked Anto. "I'm finished work at nine."
"We built the best snowman ya ever saw in your entire life at Red's so we did this mornin'," boasted Po.
"I have ta admit it's a good one," put in Topcoat.
"I'll have ta go up and see it," said Anto.
"We're all goin' there later so come up after work," suggested Topcoat.
"I'll do just that," smiled Anto.
"Hey, ya should have heard 'head the ball' here on about snowmen this mornin'. He's off his rocker so he is," laughed Topcoat pointing at Po.
"What were ya on about now?" smiled Anto at Po.
"All I did was state a fact. Not my fault that empty headed people can't accept it," said Po glaring at Topcoat.
"Ok Po, well, tell me then?"
"Well it's like this, as I'm sure you know, snowmen throughout history have been possessed by spirits."

"Now, a have ta admit that I didn't know that Po," smiled Anto.
"Well, it's the truth. They only stay a short time, just on the first night the snowman was built."
"Are ya sayin' they appear in all snowmen?" asked Anto.
"No, don't be stupid, just the odd one."
"And the one yous built is an odd one is it?" grinned Anto.
"It is, a got a feelin' about it when it was finished."
"Po, will it snow again tonight? Like since ya have your head up there in the clouds, ya should have a better idea than us," laughed Anto.
"Now you hold on a minute Mr. Smart Arse. I remember a guy who didn't believe me before and went with me ta Ballyholland. That smart arse heard a Banshee and took off like an Olympic Sprinter. Can't remember who it was, can you?" said Po grinning at Anto.
"Ah now, that was totally different. Banshees are a national belief in Ireland, sure who has ever heard of snowmen havin' spirits for God's sake?"
"That's because they have very short lives ya see. They only last a day or two then they melt."
"Aye, right," smirked Anto.
"Hey, ya don't have ta believe me, I don't care. Maybe this snowman doesn't have a spirit, but I know for sure that some of them do, and as long as I know, that's all that matters."
"Do ya believe in all this shit Topcoat?" said Anto.
"To be honest, no, a don't. But a have heard stories before about possessed snowmen out in the country."
"Ya shouldn't tempt fate Anto, ya never know. You're dealing with unknown forces," added Po pointing at Anto.
"Never happen Po, never happen," smirked Anto.

****

Po arrived at Red's house around seven that night.
"Did ya sprinkle some water on the snowman?" he asked Red.
"Yeah, it's as hard as a rock now."
"I had an idea."
"Oh God no, what?"

"Have ya a long extension lead?"
"I suppose so, why?"
Po produced two small red lights from his pocket.
"I found these in the attic, two wee night lights. If I can use them for eyes it will make the effect even better," smiled Po.
"Not a bad idea a'tall. I'll get the lead, we can plug it in the socket in the hen house."

Red and Po gently removed the back of the now, iced snowman, took out the manikin and hid it away. Po got inside the snowman and fitted perfectly. He tried out the lights that Red had connected and when lit, they made the eyes glow red.
"Well what do ya think?" Po asked standing back and looking at their work.
"I think it looks great. What are ya goin' to do when Anto's here, start groanin' or somethin'?" laughed Red.
"I'll say hello or something, scare the shit outta him."

All the gang arrived around eight o'clock and admired the finished snowman. It was now dark and Red had to put on a small light at his back door which gave quite an eerie effect further down the yard where the snowman was, causing long shadows.
"He's comin'," panted Ginger who arrived running, he had been watching for the arrival of Anto.
"Right Po, get inside, and keep the light switch in your hand. Don't put on the eyes until ya start ta speak, right?"
"Right."
The lads had lit a small fire some ten feet from the snowman which added to the atmosphere.
"Well is this himself?" asked Anto arriving.
"What do ya think?" asked Red.
"A good one for sure, yis did a hell of a job all right."
Red winked at Ginger who slipped away and went back up the yard and turned out the light. The snowman was now only dimly lit by the light of the small fire.
"He looks almost alive," commented Topcoat.
"Right, and he's goin' ta talk ta us now is he?" laughed Anto.

Suddenly a low groan came from within the snowman, it got louder. The eyes began to turn red. Anto's mouth dropped open.
"I am here," came the deep echoed voice of the snowman.
"Jasus," whispered Anto.
There was silence for a few seconds, then the night was shattered with a high pitched scream from the snowman. Everyone turned and ran at speed, or to be more precise, followed Anto. Red was the only one left. He walked around to the back of the snowman and found Po sitting on the ground.
"What the hell was that?"
"Whorin', shittin' friggin' bastard…"
"What, what?"
"The whorin' electric wire."
"What about the whorin' electric wire?"
"I nearly got electrocuted so a did."
"Ya what?" asked Red trying not to laugh.
"Ya didn't cover that friggin' lead right and a touched a bare wire, Jasus, it went right through me, thought I was finished."
Red sat down in the snow and roared.
"I'm glad ya think it's funny ya whore."
"Ya got it back ta front ya ejit, ya were supposed ta shock Anto not yourself."
"Funny, ha, ha."

No one but Topcoat and Ginger were ever told the truth of what happened. Anto believed the snowman was possessed by a tortured spirit, and insisted its heart rendering screams would stay with him forever. So, a new page was written in the history of Newry which was hereafter known as, 'The Shocking Possessed Snowman'. Of course, as Anto said, future generations would just not believe it.

End

The Conversation

1960

"Who did?"
"He did, amn't a tellin' ya?"
"And ya know this for sure?"
"Yeah."
"Jasus."
"And not a bother on him either."
"Well, wank me."
"Not a hope in Hell."
"No, what?"
"I won't wank ya."
"Piss off."
"Piss off, your own self."
"When did all this happen?"
"Yesterday."
"Does Anto know?"
"No."
"He'll shit."
"He will."
"I just can't believe it."
"Well, it happened."

"Who actually witnessed it?"
"Jumpy, Bishop, Lanky, Jammy and me own self."
"What did the Bishop say?"
"Shit."
"What?"
"He said shit, he said shit. Are ya deef, or what?"
"Frig me, don't get your knickers in a twist, and did he wait or hesitate or anythin'?"
"No, he just said shit."
"No, ya dope, I'm not talkin' about the Bishop, I'm talkin' about himself."
"Well, why didn't ya say that? Am I supposed ta read your mind?"
"Well, did he? Did he hesitate or anythin'?"
"No, just did it, no messin' about, no waitin' no hesitatin', he just did it."
"Christ, that's somethin', for sure."
"Ya should have been there, ya know."
"I wish I had been, I missed a historic event."
"Ya did."
"I did."
"Never thought anyone would ever do it, did you?"
"Not in a million years."
"What did he say afterwards?"
"Not a lot, just said he took the notion, and decided ta do it."
"Just took the notion?"
"That's what he said, so it is."
"Jasus."
"Jasus is right."
"There's cool for ya."
"I tell ya what, it took some nerve."
"Nerve? That was pure courage, so it was, he can only be admired."
"Ya know, he will be a legend in his own time now, so he will."
"That he will. I'm in shock, so a am. Just imagine, someone askin' Mary Halloran out."
"I know, I know, friggin' deadly, isn't it?"

End

The Matchmaker

1960

"Po, that's a load of shit."
"Ya do, ya fancy her, Red. Sure, a know ya do."
"No, I don't."
"Sure ya do, I saw the way ya looked at her."
"I don't look at her any different than I look at any other girl."
"Is that so? Then ya look at Mary Halloran the same way, do ya?"
"No, but that's different."
"How?"
"It just is."
"What ya mean is, ya don't fancy Mary Halloran, right?"
"Of course I don't fancy Mary Halloran, but that has nothin' ta do with it."
"So what's the difference, then?"
"What are ya talkin' about?"
"Well, if ya look at your one this way, and ya look at another one another way, what's the difference?"
"You are tryin' ta muddy the waters, so ya are."
"I'm just askin' a simple question."
"Look, I said I didn't fancy her, that's it."

"I see."
"Do ya?"
"Do I what?"
"See!"
"I see you're all mixed up and won't admit it."
"Mixed up about what?"
"Your one."
"What one?"
"The one ya fancy but won't admit it."
"I told ya already, I don't fancy her."
"So ya don't like her legs then?"
"I didn't say that."
"So, ya do like her legs then."
"She has nice legs, so what?"
"Ah, I see, it's her yokes ya don't like?"
"I didn't say that either, she has really nice breasts."
"I knew it, it's her face, right?"
"No, she has a very pretty face."
"She has lovely eyes, doesn't she?"
"Yeah, she has."
"And a beautiful smile."
"Yeah, she has."
"And a fantastic bum."
"Definitely fantastic."
"Ok, so, she has nice legs, nice breasts, a lovely face, lovely eyes, a lovely smile, fantastic bum, but ya don't fancy her?"
"Right."
"Friggin' liar."
"No, I'm not. Can I not think a girl is nice without fancyin' her?"
"But ya think she is beautiful."
"So?"
"Ya should hear what she says about you."
"What does she say about me?"
"Can't tell ya."
"Why?"
"Well, sure ya don't fancy her, so what difference does it make?"
"That's not the point."

"Ah, I see. So I should tell ya what she said, break my word ta her, just for you, who doesn't even fancy her?"

"But let's say, just for the craic now, that I did fancy her, just speakin' hypothetically, like."

"Ok, so, hypothetically I might tell ya what she said."

"Right, so, if I fancied her, hypothetically speakin', ok, ya would tell me what she said about me?"

"No."

"Jasus Christ, sure ya just said ya would."

"It would be hypothetically unethical."

"You are full ta the neck with shit."

"Maybe, but now, if ya fancied her, now that would be a different matter."

"How?"

"Well, it would be ok to tell someone that fancied someone else what someone else said if in the first place that someone fancied the other someone, ya see."

"What?"

"I think ya fancy her far too much ta understand the subtlety of love."

"You're off your friggin' head."

"Then again, if it was a date ya were wantin' with her that might be a different thing."

"Now, hold on a minute. Are ya sayin' that ya can arrange a date with her?"

"Maybe."

"So, if I were ta arrange, through you, ta go out with her, ya would tell me what she said?"

"It's possible."

"Ok, then."

"Ok, then what?"

"Make a date with her for me."

"Ok."

"Will she go out with me?"

"She might."

"Will ya tell me now what she said about me?"

"I just might."

"Tell me, ya wee whore."

"First, will ya meet her Friday night at 8pm outside the Florentine Café?"
"I will."
"I'd already arranged it."
"Did anyone ever tell ya how much of a bastard ya are?"
"I get all sorts of compliments."
"Now, what did she say about me then?"
"She said she didn't fancy ya."
"She did? I knew she liked me. Brilliant."
"One does one's best."

End

Shark Fishing in Newry Canal

1960

"So where are yous goin' later?" Jumpy asked Red and Po as they stood outside Uncle Luigi's on Hill Street. Jumpy's mate Dunno was there also.
"Down ta the canal," answered Po.
"Just for a walk like?" asked Dunno.
"No Dunno, don't be silly, we're goin' shark fishing so we are," said a straight faced Po.
"Yeah, right, de ya think we're stupid? There are no sharks in Newry Canal," laughed Jumpy.
Po looked at Red.
"See, didn't I tell ya, not everybody knows about the sharks in the canal."
"How could sharks get into the canal for God's sake?" continued Jumpy still laughing.
"How do the boats get in? Through the locks of course," Po was still maintaining a straight face.

"Naw, yous are havin' me on so ya are," said Dunno with an unsure smile.
"Look, I don't care if ya believe us or not. We're goin' shark fishin' this afternoon. If we get one, Anto has agreed ta pay us £5 for it," put in Red.
Just then Anto appeared as if on cue at the door.
"Anto, de ya know what these two are trying ta tell us?"
"Po's brother is really his sister?" smiled Anto.
"No, they're tryin' to say there's sharks in the canal."
"And...?" replied Anto quick as a flash.
"It's a joke isn't it?"
"What, about the sharks in the canal? Ya wouldn't think it was funny if one of them got a hold a ya," said Anto seriously.
Dunno and Jumpy exchanged glances.
"This is for real now, no messin'," said Jumpy.
"Look, Jumpy, if ya don't want ta believe us, don't. I don't care. There's the man standin' there that'll tell ya. If we get one he is goin' ta give us £5 for it so he is," said Red.
"Can we go with ya?" asked Dunno.
"I can't stop ya, but as long as ya stay outta the way. And if we catch a shark don't think you're gettin' any money outta it."

Later that afternoon the two shark fishermen and the two shark fishermen observers arrived at a prearranged spot just past Dromalane Housing Estate. Red and Po got their rods and hooks organised and began fishing.
"Them wee hooks would never catch a shark Po," sneered Jumpy.
"Jasus Jumpy de ya think we're stupid do ya, worse than that de ya think the sharks are stupid? Sure we don't want them ta know we're fishing for them do we?"
"Never thought of that," said Jumpy apologetically.

Sometime later, the two observers had wandered a few yards away from the shark fishermen to investigate something they noticed floating in the water.
"Did ya get the stuff?" whispered Red.

Po produced a small bottle from his pocket. Red had to cover his face to make sure the two boys did not hear him laughing.
"How will ya do it then?" whispered Red.
"See that big stone there, well, you get them distracted and I'll throw it in."
"Brilliant," smirked Red.
Just then an Ice Cream van pulled up beside them. It was Anto and his Uncle Roberto. Anto got out first and approached Red.
"Any big fellas yet?"
"Not yet," smiled Red. "But a have a feelin' one will be here very soon."
Anto moved closer and whispered, "When I told Roberto what yous had convinced them two ejits of, he had ta come ta see it for himself."
"Ya couldn't have timed it better Anto. Will ya go down there ta them two and distract them for a few minutes and when I shout, make it look good."
"I will, I will," said Anto as he moved off.
"Well lads, what's happening?" asked Anto as he approached Dunno and Jumpy.
"Frig all, no sharks that's for sure," smiled Jumpy.
"Ah sure ya have ta give them time ya know," said Anto with conviction.
Suddenly there was a great splash somewhere beside Po.
"Ahaaaaa," screamed Po loudly as he rolled on the canal bank.
"Jasus Christ, did ya see that?" exclaimed Anto.
Anto and the two boys ran toward Red and Po.
Po was still rolling on the ground in apparent agony.
"Jasus did ya see it Anto, it was a friggin' monster," panted Red excitedly.
"Are ya all right Po?" asked Roberto who had now emerged from the van.
"It got ma hand," screamed Po.
He held up an empty sleeve which was covered in dripping blood and said again…
"It got ma hand."
"Jasus, we better get him to hospital before he bleeds ta death," suggested Roberto.

Dunno bent forward to see Po's wound. When he saw the blood he, without a word, slowly sunk to the ground with eyes closed, white as a sheet in a dead faint.
Red was having difficulty now keeping his face straight. Jumpy's shaking of Dunno was beginning to have an effect. He was starting to come around. By now Roberto had Po in the back of the van and was making a great deal of hurrying the whole process.
"Will you lads be ok? We'll have ta get Po ta hospital," shouted Anto.
"Yeah, you go on ahead, we'll make our own way back," replied Red.

Later that night everyone in Uncle Luigi's knew about the great shark attack on poor Po. The two lads Dunno and Jumpy never had so much attention in their lives.
Then, in walks Red with Po closely following.
The two boys ran to see Po as he sat down in the middle snug.
"Po, are ya all right?" asked Jumpy with some passion.
"Back as good as new," smiled Po showing two hands to Jumpy.
"Jasus Christ…look Dunno, he's got his hand back."
"Frig me, that's somethin' else that is."
"Some fisherman caught the shark ten minutes after we left and got my hand back, they sewed it back on at the hospital so they did."
Jumpy looked at Dunno and back at Po. Red could no longer hold on, he burst into laughter as did everyone else in the café.
"Ah Jasus, ya bastards, ya took us for a ride so ya did," said Jumpy.
"And all that blood too, made me sick so it did. Where did ya get it?" added Dunno.
"The joke shop, where else?" laughed Po.
"Jasus," they both exclaimed together.
"By the way lads, are yous doin' anythin' tomorrow?" asked Red.
"Dunno looked at Jumpy.
"No, don't think so, why?"
"Well Po and myself are goin' whale fishin' out in Camlough Lake if ya wanna come?"

End

The Toffee Apple Conspiracy

1960

"Well sure I sat and scoffed eight toffee apples one after the other," said Boots Markey.
"Your arse in parsley Boots. There's no way ya ate that many toffee apples, no way," jumped in Po.
"No bother ta me. I could eat twice that many, not a problem ta me."
"Boots, ya talk some shit so ya do," laughed Jumpy.
"I'm not talkin' shit so I'm not. I am the best toffee apple eater in this town, if not all Ireland," boasted Boots.
"Now that's a challenge if I ever heard one," said Red.
"Again, not a bother."
"Well Po, what de ya say. Will ya take him on?"
"The toffee apple competition is now officially a go," smiled Po.
"Right, let's go and see Anto."

All three explained the challenge to Anto at the counter of Uncle Luigi's.
"Sounds like a goer ta me for sure. Are yous havin' a private bet?"

"Well, Boots is the great boaster, so what do ya say, how much?"
Boots rubbed his chin.
"How does a fiver sound?"
"Sounds all right ta me," quipped Po.
"Right, I'll set up the day and time then, right?" said Anto.
Both agreed.
When Boots had left the café they all sat down in one of the snugs and the real planning was under way.
"Jasus that Boots fella needs ta be taken down a peg so he does," commented Red.
"And we're the ones ta do it. Now, needless ta say, ya have ta win this Po. If I am goin' to set up a book on it I want ta be sure we'll come out on top," continued Anto.
"We need some way ta make sure that Boots can't finish, or drops out," said Po.
"That's it, so any ideas?" asked Red.
"I have a question, where are the toffee apples comin' from?" asked Anto.
"Never thought of that," mused Red.
"Don't worry, I know how ta make them anyway," said Anto.
"Ok then we will leave that part of it with your own self," added Red.
"That's it Anto, since you are goin' ta be makin' the toffee apples ya can find some way ta make sure the ones he eats don't go down too well."
"Good idea, leave it with me for now, I'll come up with somethin'."

****

A week passed and the day Anto arranged for the toffee apple eating competition arrived. He chose a Tuesday as his Uncles Luigi and Roberto always went to another member of the family in Portadown to play poker on that night every week. All the gang had gathered out the back of the café and Anto had made a large lot of toffee apples which were laid out on two trays, one in front of each of the contestants.
"Now, when I say go, ya both will start eatin' right?" said Anto to both contestants.
"Waste of time, ya should just give up now Po," smirked Boots.
"We'll see," snapped back Po straight faced.

"Ready, steady…Go!"

Both started eating with relish to the encouragement of both sets of supporters. Five minutes later, both were on their fourth toffee apple but Boots seemed to be slowing. Half way through the fifth, Boots suddenly stood up and took off at speed in the direction of the toilets. "I hereby declare Po Hillen to be Newry's Champion Toffee Apple Eater," said Anto raising Po's arm in the air to cheers and applause from his supporters.

Later Po, Anto and Red were sitting having some coffee in the front snug.
"Well give us the inside story Anto," said Red.
"Simple really when I thought about it. When I was making the toffee apples, I divided them into two lots and in one lot I put in a few large spoonfuls of what Uncle Luigi calls his jollop powder with the toffee. He takes it for bad constipation. It works very fast so it does."
"Cute," laughed Red.
"Well poor Boots took off fast for sure."
"That he did," laughed Anto. "After all ya can't hold what ya haven't got in your hand."

End

The Super Leprechaun

1960

The gang were sitting in a circle on the grass at the back of Red's house on Castle Street engrossed in a discussion about the movies.
"The problem is you're biased against British movies so ya are Po," said Topcoat.
"No I'm not. Look, when ya see a movie made in Hollywood there are ordinary people in it. In the British movies most of them are all…'I say old chap' types."
"He's right ya know Topcoat, most British films are about middle or upper class people," added Jumpy Jones.
"Well, that may be the case but at least they don't think we're idiots like the Americans do," said Red.
"Why de ya say that?" asked Anto.
"Well, take Superman. He saves the world and then changes back into Clark Kent, but no one recognises him because he wears this fantastic disguise…a pair of glasses."
This caused a giggle amongst the group.
"He's right," laughed Anto. "Sure the Lone Ranger is as bad…his disguise is a wee mask."
"Which is a wee bit better than Superman's for sure," laughed Ginger.

"But at least he changes his clothes," added Po. "The Lone Ranger wears the same clothes everyday, he even sleeps in them every night... he would find it hard ta hide from the Indians, they could smell him at a hundred yards."

This caused another round of giggles and laughs.

"But ya have ta admit that his gun is great. He never has ta reload. He can fire hundreds of bullets without havin' ta reload," said Topcoat.

"Yeah, never thought of that," laughed Red.

"Sure Tonto's the same, he wears the same clothes all the time too," said Anto.

"Can ya imagine what their socks would smell like?" asked Ginger making a face.

"Yep, just like Po's," laughed Red who got himself a kick on the shin from Po for his effort.

"And here's another one, ya know when Clark Kent changes into Superman in the phone box, where does his clothes go?" asked Ginger.

"Hey, never thought of that," mused Red.

"Ok, I have one...Tarzan, why does he never grow a beard? Like he would hardly have a razor in the jungle would he?" laughed Anto.

"Well done Anto...so why does he not have a beard...anyone know?" asked Red.

Head shaking was his only answer.

"There's no doubt about it, Hollywood must think we're idiots," said Anto.

"It's not us they think are idiots," put in Po. "It's the Americans their own selves they think are idiots."

"Why's that?" asked Topcoat.

"Well, think about it. Superman says he stands for 'Truth, Justice and the American Way'. So it's the Americans the whole thing is aimed at."

This got another giggle.

"What we need is an Irish Hero, what de ya think?" spouted up Anto.

"I agree," said Red. "I vote for Topcoat."

This caused loud cheering.

"Piss off ya bunch a weirdos," sneered Topcoat.

"I stand for 'Free Ice Cream, Naked Women, No Cops, Loads of Fags and the Irish Way," said Po with seriousness. This got him a warm round of applause.
"We will have to design a special suit for him," said Anto rubbing his chin.
"It will have ta be green of course," added Red.
"Goes without sayin'," put in Anto.
"He can wear it under his topcoat, and when he is needed to save someone he just throws off the auld topcoat and races to the rescue," put in Po.
"Well, I see him in the green suit, orange knickers and a white cloak," added Jumpy.
"Correct and right, a super hero like Topcoat would have to be dressed in the Irish colours."
"What will he be called?" asked Red.
"How about 'Supercoat'," suggested Jumpy.
"Naw, don't like that one. How about 'Super Leprechaun'?" suggested Red.
"That's the one," laughed Po.
"I'll get our one ta run up a suit for Topcoat so a will, she's a dab hand at the sewin' machine thing," said Po later to Red.
"Excellent idea, de ya know we will have ta get him ta save a life ta break in the new suit Po, ya'll have ta think of somethin'."
"Don't worry, I'll come up with somethin'."

****

With a lot of begging, pleading, stealing and promises, the material and all the accessories were finally found and the suit made. The day for the big suit fitting arrived. It was decided to have this great event at the back of Uncle Luigi's. All the usual crowd were there for the show. Topcoat used Anto's room to change and arrived at the back of the café to tumultuous applause.
"Jasus Topcoat, ya look the part," laughed Anto.
"A true Super Leprechaun for sure," added Po.
Topcoat did a few twirls in his new green suit enjoying his moment of fame.

Jammy McAteer ran in, seemingly out of breath.
"Jasus lads, one of the girls has had a wagon fall on her, round in Water Street, an we can't move it."
Without a word everyone raced out the back of Uncle Luigi's onto Mill Street and around the corner onto Water Street. There they came across the scene of a large cart lying on its side.
Underneath they could see a pair of woman's legs in black woollen stockings. Standing around were a few of the girls who were regulars in Uncle Luigi's all crying and pleading for someone to help. The boys arrived and Anto quickly took charge of the situation.
"Right Topcoat, we'll go around to the side of the cart and lift. When we get it up enough, pull her out, right?"
"Right," said Topcoat still panting from his running.
The boys began lifting the cart and it started to move. Topcoat grabbed the girl's legs around the ankles and began to pull as hard as he could. Suddenly the legs were free and with nothing holding them anymore Topcoat lost his balance and fell backwards with a surprised look on his face and a leg in each hand.
A cheer went up from everyone there.
A couple of the girls ran over to Topcoat and began hugging and kissing him on the cheeks.
"My hero," said one.
"A true Super Leprechaun," cried the other.
Topcoat sat up and looked at the two manikin legs in his hands.
"Yous dirty whorin' bastards," he yelled, which only added to the gang's amusement.
"I should 'a known so a should."
The boys all reached the safety of the cafe without any of them having their heads split open by the two flailing legs being wielded by a screaming Super Leprechaun.

End

The Parochial Hall

1960

Red, Po and Dunno were sitting on the steps of the central street lamp in Market Street.

"Are ya goin' ta the Parochial on Saturday night?" asked Dunno.

"I hate goin' ta that place," answered Red.

"Me too," put in Po.

"Why, I thought ya loved goin'?"

"I love the bands they get, its them stupid priests that do ma head in."

"That's my answer too…it's that Father Heffernan…he's the worst. How could anyone enjoy a dance with him and his stupid ruler walking around the floor like Hitler?"

Just then Joey Thomson and Kitter arrived and sat down.

"What's the craic?"

"We were just talkin' about the Parochial and the stupid priests," said Po.

"What about them…I've never been to the Parochial before, but I heard its good," said Joey.

"That's right, you're a Protestant, but sure a lot of Prods go," said Dunno.

"I know, I'm goin' ta go when the Miami Showband is on again."
"Well we were just sayin' it would be a great place ta go if it wasn't for the stupid priests," said Red.
"Why, what's wrong with the priests?" asked Joey.
"Well, take this Father Heffernan. He walks around all night. When the slow dances are playin' he gets out his stupid ruler. If ya'r dancin' too close to a girl…he pushes ya apart and puts the ruler against her stomach and says…'no closer than twelve inches'," complained Red angrily.
"Yous are havin' me on," laughed Joey.
"Ask anybody, I swear ta God, this is what he does," went on Red. "And that's not the worst, see if ya click with a bird and take her up to the balcony for a Coke, well, sure isn't his nibs up there every ten minutes checkin' if ya have your arm round her," snarled Red.
"Jasus, that's weird."
"Weird? Po, tell him about Jimmy Havern last month."
"Christ, nearly forgot about that. Jimmy was sittin' up on the balcony with his girlfriend. He was givin' her a wee kiss when the demon in black arrived behind them. He grabbed them by the scruff of the neck and put them out."
"If it wasn't for the bands I wouldn't go near the place," added Red.
"Now I'm havin' second thoughts about goin' there a'tall," mused Joey.
"Wouldn't blame ya Joey. What's your crowd like?"
"Not too bad really, well…not as bad as the priests for sure, but that doesn't mean I would sit in our church hall and snog some bird," laughed Joey.
"Well sure come with us on Sunday night then," suggested Red. "The Royal is playin'."
"I'd love ta," replied Joey.

As good as his word, Joey turned up to meet Red and Po and went with them to the Parochial Hall. During the dance Red had got himself a girl called Kathleen O'Hara, a tall, slim, very pretty dark haired girl that came from a little village outside Newry called Bessbrook. They were sitting on the balcony having a milkshake when Joey arrived with a girl called Mary McShane, who Red knew.

"That is some band," said Joey sitting down beside Red.
"That they are. Hi Mary. What are ya doin' with this ugly 'head the ball'? I thought ya had better taste than that."
"Did I ever go out with you Red Morgan?"
"No."
"There ya are then, that proves a have good taste."
Red turned and looked at Joey.
"De ya hear the cheek of that one Joey. Tongue as sharp as a knife. Don't believe a word that comes outta her mouth. She has asked me out more times that I've had hot dinners."
This got Red a bang on the leg with Mary's shoe.
Red moaned and rubbed his leg.
"Ya didn't hit him half hard enough Mary," laughed Kathleen.

After a bit more banter, both Red and Joey turned their conversation to their respective partners. They both were sitting with their arms around the girl's shoulders.
"And what in God's name do you two gentlemen think you are doing?" came the booming voice of Father Heffernan from behind them.
They all turned around quickly and looked up at the priest. No one spoke.
"Are you all deaf?" continued the priest.
"We're not doin' anything Father," Red managed to get out.
"You're Morgan aren't you?"
"Yes Father."
"You should know better, behaving in public like animals."
"What did you say?" asked Joey standing up.
"Behaving like crude animals I said, like dogs on the street. Who are you to answer me back?"
"Who are you to speak to us like that? There are two ladies sitting here who I am sure do not want to be listenin' to your vulgar innuendoes. Did no one ever bother to teach you how to speak in front of ladies or is it you just have no manners?"
"I will see you at the Parochial House tomorrow, you impudent brat, at three sharp," growled Father Heffernan, the veins standing out on his neck.
"No ya won't," spat back Joey.

"What?"
"You will not see me at the Parochial House tomorrow or any other day. I, and all my family are members of the Church of Ireland. Our ministers do not speak to their parishioners in such ignorant terms. My father is a Magistrate here in Newry and when I go home I will relay to him the way you have insulted myself, my friend and these two ladies. Knowing my father, who has no time for bullies, I think he will take a long look at your entertainment licence."
Red looked at Father Heffernan's face. It was getting redder and redder. He thought a vein would burst at any second. The priest growled something inaudible and stormed off.
"I never thought I would see the day," exclaimed Red excitedly.
"What?" asked Joey sitting down again.
"Someone puttin' Father Heffernan in his box. Jasus Christ, well done Joey ma lad," laughed Red patting Joey's back. "Are ya really goin' ta tell your da?"
"Are ya outta your skull? My da's a painter with the council. If a told him what I just done he'd bate the shit clean outta me."
The two girls and Red burst into sustained laughter.
"Well done Joey," gasped Red putting his arm around his friend's shoulders. "I never thought I'd say the words, but, it's a big one up, for the Prods."

End

The Pen Pal

1960

Red was lying on his bed reading the latest Topper comic when he heard Po's voice downstairs. A few moments later Po entered the room.
"Well bucket head."
"Afternoon fartface."
"De ya remember me tellin' ya about ma pen pal from India?"
"Yeah."
"Guess what, he's coming here on holiday."
"To Newry?"
"Well he's goin' ta his cousin's in London for two weeks and he's comin' here ta stay with me so he is for a weekend. He's arrivin' in London on Tuesday next."
"Ya lookin' forward ta seein' him?"
"Yeah, course a am, great, isn't it?"
"Suppose."
"He's a really nice guy so he is…sure ya know that…ya've read some of his letters."
"Well ya better start plannin' then."
"Plannin'?"

"Well a mean, what will ya do with him for a whole weekend? Ya'll have to plan ta take him places. De ya want ta spend the whole time sittin' in Uncle Luigi's?"
"Ya'r right ya know, put up ya'r right hand."
"What for?"
"Put it up ya swine," said Po as he grabbed Red's right arm and pulled it upwards.
"What, what?"
"I hereby swear you in as Deputy Pen Pal Entertainments Manager."
"Ya can piss away off Po."
"Ach Red, ya'll have ta help me out here. I told him ya were ma best friend, that ya were a really nice guy, that ya would do anythin' for me, ya know, lies like that."
"Well, we'll have ta get the whole gang in on it ta help."
"Good idea,"

The next two weeks passed quickly and the day arrived when Po's friend was due. Po was banging on Red's door that morning before nine o'clock.
"What are ya doing here at this time on a Saturday morning ya wee gobshite?"
"He's arrivin' at eleven on the Belfast bus."
"That's two hours away Po."
"Well, sure the bus is early sometimes isn't it?"
"Not two friggin' hours early."
"Are ya makin' the tae?"
"Jasus, toast some bread will ya?"

At eleven o'clock Red and Po were sitting on the Clanrye River wall that runs the length of the Mall.
"What's his name again?" asked Red.
"Don't be askin' me that, I can't pronounce it."
"Well what will I call him then?"
"Charlie."
"Charlie?"
"Charlie."
"Weird name for an Indian."

Just then the Belfast express pulled in.
"How will we know him?" asked Red.
"Good question Red, never thought of that. Everybody on the bus will be coloured and from India."
"Jasus ya'r a real smart arse this mornin' aren't ya?"
The passengers were now disembarking and Po spotted his friend.
He was a tall, lean, quite good looking boy who looked older than his fifteen years.
"Hello…Charlie?" said Po approaching him.
"Oliver?"
"Yeah…this is Red."
"Hello Red, Oliver has told me a lot about you," said Charlie shaking hands warmly.
"Well, it's probably all lies anyway," smiled Red. He turned to Po and whispered, "Oliver?"
His answer was a sharp elbow in the ribs.
Red and Po helped Charlie with his bags and began walking along the Mall towards Po's house which was only a short distance away.
"So, we call ya Charlie then?" asked Red.
"Yes, Charlie will do very fine."
"Why Charlie? That's an English name."
"My Indian name is not easy to pronounce."
"What is it?" pressed Red.
"Manishankar Rajkumar."
"Ok, Charlie it is then."
They all laughed.
"You speak very good English," said Red.
"Thank you, I have been learning English for many years, it is our second language. Do you speak any other languages?"
"Still tryin' to get ta grips with the English," laughed Red feeling a little embarrassed. "We do take French at school, I suppose at a push I could order fish and chips in Paris."

They arrived at Po's house where Charlie was introduced to everyone and a great fuss was made getting him settled in and comfortable. Later all three ended up at Uncle Luigi's. Charlie was introduced to the gang

and was warmly welcomed especially by the girls who spent their time whispering and giggling.
"So…what have ya planned for the rest of the day?" asked Anto.
"Nothin' a'tall. Charlie just wanted to wander around and see the town."
"Where did ya take him?" asked Jumpy.
"Showed him the Town Hall first, he liked that, didn't ya Charlie."
"Truly marvellous indeed, the idea of building it, on a bridge, very unique."
"The rest of the time we just wandered about the town and through the market."
"It is a very nice town you live in," remarked Charlie.
"What did ya like best?" asked Anto.
"These fish and chips are top of my list so far, but you have beautiful girls in Newry," smiled Charlie showing well cared for white teeth.
Anto looked across at the table Charlie was looking at.
"I wouldn't go as far as beautiful Charlie, but a couple of them would do if ya were stuck I suppose," laughed Anto.
"Tell ya what Charlie," butted in Jumpy, "How would ya like to go ta a Record Hop tonight?"
"What is a Record Hop?" asked Charlie.
"You've never been ta a Record Hop?" gasped Jumpy.
"I do not think so, what is it?"
"They have a guy, a DJ, who plays all the latest records ya see, and we all get up and dance. An all them beautiful women will be there too."
"Ah, I understand. Yes I would like to go to your Record Hop," smiled Charlie.

That evening the gang and Charlie went to the Record Hop at The Bucket on Castle Street. Charlie was of course the centre of attention for all the girls there. He was a pretty good dancer as well and found himself up on the dance floor for most of the night. If there was one thing that could be said about the girls at the Bucket Record Hop, it would be that they were not backward about coming forward. Poor Charlie was up for almost every dance not wanting to insult any of the girls by saying no thank you. By the end of the night he had made three dates, had agreed to meet two others for coffee during the day and was invited to a Birthday Party.

The highlight of Charlie's short holiday came the following night. He had a date with Noreen Dillan.
"She is such a lovely girl, that Noreen," mused Charlie as he sat with Red, Po and Anto in Uncle Luigi's.
"Lovely, well a suppose she's not bad lookin', but she has a tongue on her that would sharpen pencils," commented Anto.
"What is this pencil sharpening?" Charlie asked.
This brought a round of laughter from his three friends.
"It means ya wouldn't wanna be fallin' out with her. She has what we call a sharp tongue," laughed Red.
"Ah, I understand," smiled Charlie.
"Where are ya gonna take her?" asked Po.
"I don't know, where do you suggest?"
"Well, there's the Pictures."
"Pictures?"
"Cinema."
"Right, Cinema."
"Or ya could take her for a walk?" suggested Red.
"I think Cinema would be best and then perhaps we can get something to eat afterwards."
"He's no slouch this Charlie fella, he knows the ropes," smiled Anto.

Charlie arranged to meet up with the boys at the end of the night at the café. When he arrived the café was closed, all the cleaning had been done and the gang were sitting in the first snug eating their chips. He was let in by Anto and when seated was cross questioned by the lads on his date with Noreen.
"A very strange girl I think," mused Charlie.
"Strange? How?" asked Red.
"I was leaving her home and just before we got there we were talking about girl's figures. She asked me if I liked her legs. I said I did, very much and that I thought she had a nice fanny and that next time I came to visit I would take her somewhere nice for a ride," said Charlie
Everyone at the table was roaring with laughter.

"Did I do wrong perhaps?"
"What did she say?" Po managed to get out.
"She slapped my face, went into her house and slammed the door!"
When everyone quietened down Red put his hand on Charlie's shoulder.
"No Charlie, ya said nothin' wrong. I suppose ya could put it down to an international language misunderstanding," smiled Red.
"I do not understand."
"Well, where do a start, ya see, here, fanny does not mean, bum. It means the other bit on the front, ya understand?"
"Oh dear, I think I am beginning to."
"Secondly, having a ride with a girl is not taking her for a drive, but having sex with her," laughed Red.
"Oh my goodness. I will be arrested and put in jail," moaned Charlie with his head in his hands.
"No ya won't Charlie, don't be silly, it was just a mix up," put in Po.
They managed to get Charlie settled down.
"And you said Red that my English was very good did you not? It is not so good I think."
"Your English is fine, it's just that we have different meanings for some words here, that's all."

Charlie caught his bus back to the airport on the Monday morning and was seen off by about six of the gang. He promised to write to everyone. He insisted that Po send him a list of what he called 'double words' so he would not ever make such a mistake again.

Charlie went on to become a doctor and ended up working at one of London's top hospitals. For many years he and Po continued to communicate. Po, being Po, never ever let him forget his gaff while he was in Newry on holiday that first time. He always started his letters, 'Dear Fanny'.

End

A Day Out for 3C

1960

"Now before we go I am going to give you all one final warning. I want you to be on your best behaviour at all times. You are to stay together, no wandering off. You will walk in twos and make sure you all have your note books and pencils with you. Does everyone understand?"
"Yes Sir," replied 3C in one voice.

Mr. Gains was a small, thin man, with sharp features. His black receding hair perhaps made him look older than he in fact was. He had dreaded this outing all week from the moment he was first informed by the Head Master that he would be taking 3C, with Mr. Sweeney, to Daisy Hill Nursery, a local Botanical Garden.

Mr. Sweeney arrived and leaned over to speak to Mr. Gains out of the earshot of 3C.
"Are you ready for this?"
"No, how could anyone be ready for 3C? It's a disaster in the making. I can feel it in my bones. Just think of 3C, all 33 of them, with two teachers? It's madness I tell you, madness."

"I was thinking the same thing. I was trying to think what I've done on himself in the office to get this job."
"We should have had at least an armed squad of police with us you know," Mr. Gains managed a nervous smile.
"Even with that I wouldn't have felt comfortable. Well, I suppose it's time to take the plunge, onwards and upwards. Gird up the loins and best foot forward and all that," smiled Mr. Sweeney.

They were gathered at the front of St. Joseph's Intermediate School on Newry's Armagh Road.
"Right boys, get into a line of twos now," Mr. Gains said to a noisy 3C who all seemed to be talking at once.
"Quiet! Now line up," roared Mr. Gains.
Fifteen minutes later 3C had made it to Daisy Hill Nurseries. None of them were missing, none had been knocked down, there were no disagreements and the class was intact. The first miracle of the day had been granted. Just inside the gates Mr. Gains stopped and told 3C to have their notebooks ready to write down information about the plants which they would be asked about later in a test.
"Daisy Hill Nurseries was founded by Thomas Smith in 1887," said Mr. Gains in a loud voice.
"Was he anything ta your man Smith that played centre forward for England a long time ago?" asked Blackie, "Ma da told me about him so he did, he scored some great goals."
"No, no. Now pay attention. Thomas Smith was a botanist who…"
"What was he Sir?"
"A botanist Jones, he studied plant life and…"
"Why did he do that Sir?" asked Red.
"McManus, get down from that tree immediately," roared Mr. Sweeney to Dunno who had managed to get himself almost half way up a tall oak tree. Dunno did what he was told and even managed to do his Tarzan call on the way down to a round of applause from his laughing classmates. This however, did not deter Mr. Sweeney from connecting with Dunno's right ear.

They were halfway around the nurseries with Mr. Gains pointing out exotic plants, flowers and trees for 3C's edification. Suddenly, the

colour of Mr. Gains face seemed to change as did his expression to one of horror.
"McShane, what have you got in your hand?"
"A wee flower Sir."
"A wee flower, bring that here, now."
Mr. Gains took the flower from Shifty. The wrinkles on his face seemed to have deepened. He briefly showed it to an on looking Mr. Sweeney.
"Oh my God, he picked a 'Pacific Alabaster' orchid," groaned Mr. Gains. "McShane, do you know how valuable and rare these flowers are?"
"I liked the colour of it Sir so I picked it for my mom. She likes flowers."
Mr. Sweeney put his hand over his mouth and turned away as if to inspect another part of the nursery.
"You idiot, I told you not to touch any of the plants here."
"But Sir, I just touched it and it sort of fell off into my hand."
"You are on Head Masters Report McShane. When Mr. Ferron gets through with you, I think you will be lucky if your hands don't fall off."
"Ah that's not right, just for a wee stupid flower."
"Ahaaaaa," came the roar from the back of the group.
"Who's that?" responded Mr. Sweeney.
"I got stung by a bee Sir," complained Jumpy.
"Where?"
"Over here Sir."
"Where did you get stung Jones?"
"Here Sir, it's awful sore so it is," said Jumpy rubbing his backside.
"How on earth could a bee get into your trousers Jones?"
"Don't mind him Sir, it wasn't a bee a'tall so it wasn't," put in Boots.
"Well what happened to him Markey?"
"For God's sake Sir sure I just had this pin in ma hand and Jones sorta backed inta it."
"Sir?"
"What Morgan?"
"I think Ginger's not here. I was lookin' for him just now and he's gone."

Mr Gains looked around the group.
"Have any of you seen McVerry?" he asked.
"I did Sir," answered Blackie .
"Where?"
"He was in front of me as we lined up at the school Sir."
Mr. Sweeney intervened.
"Have any of you seen him in this past ten minutes, or since we came into the nursery?"
"I saw him lookin' at the big oak tree."
"When?"
"Few minutes ago Sir."
"Who are ya lookin' for Sir," came the voice of Ginger from behind Mr. Sweeney.
"McVerry, where were you?"
"Here Sir."
"Didn't you hear that we were looking for you?"
"No Sir, sure standin' back here I couldn't hear right Sir."
"Can we please get on now. Everyone stay together. I want you all where I can see you."
3C all bunched together ready for the next exciting moment on plant education.
"Now we will go this way, follow me," said Mr. Gains as he walked forward along the narrow path at the head of the group. No one moved. He turned around and repeated his order to 3C.
"I said follow me 3C."
"Can't Sir," spoke up Red.
"Why is that Morgan?"
"Ya told us to all stay together Sir. If we do that we wouldn't fit on the path Sir."
Mr Gains placed a hand on his forehead as if to relieve a terrible headache.
"Just go in twos please," he said in a now tired voice.

Soon they had reached the top of the hill and stopped before a great tree.
"Now, gather round 3C. This is a Redwood tree. Note how big it is. These are magnificent, stately and powerful trees. Some of them are

ancient, perhaps the oldest trees on earth. They can grow to almost four hundred feet in height, and at the base, they can be well over twenty feet wide. Their name is Sequoia Semperviren, write that down."
There was much industry now among 3C, all writing in their note books, after of course, help from Mr. Sweeney with some spellings.
"This is of course a very young tree, perhaps only a mere hundred years old," added Mr. Gains. "The average age for one of these trees is six hundred years but it has been known for some of them to be as old as two thousand years and consider, they grow from the same size as the seed inside a tomato."
"Wow," exclaimed Jumpy. "They would be as old as Mr. Gray."
"Don't be stupid Jumpy, they're not that old."
"That's enough impertinence from you boys, shut up."
"Yes Sir," answered the giggling Red and Jumpy.

When at last they had almost reached the exit gate, both Mr. Sweeney and Mr. Gains counted heads to ensure none of 3C was missing.
"Shit," came the voice of Ginger from the middle of some sort of activity at the back of the group.
"McVerry, what sort of language is that to use?" snarled Mr. Sweeney.
"What Sir?"
"I think I warned you before about using foul language McVerry."
"But sure I just said shit Sir."
"That's not a nice word to use McVerry."
"Sorry Sir. Blackie has fallen into that stuff that comes outta cow's arses."
"What?" roared Mr. Gains, quickly moving to where Ginger was pointing.
He found Blackie trying to brush himself off while standing in a great pile of steaming manure to the howls and laughter of 3C.

Mr. Gains turned to Mr. Sweeney who had arrived beside him.
"Did I perhaps make an understatement this morning saying this would be a disaster?"
Mr. Sweeney didn't reply. He just shook his head.
"Well I'm not walkin' beside him Sir," complained Red holding his nose.

"Me neither," added Jumpy.
"Jasus," complained Blackie, "I'm covered in shit."
"Fertilizer Havern, fertilizer," put in Mr. Gains quickly.
"Yes Sir, I'm covered in this fertilizer shit Sir."
"Sir?"
"What now Jones?"
"There's a creepy crawly thing behind Morgan."
"That's Kitter ya auld ejit," said Jammy.
"Oh, right, so it is," laughed Jumpy.
"Sir can we come back here again, I didn't get ta see everything?"
"No," came the voices of Mr. Sweeney and Mr. Gains.

So ended yet another day in the life of 3C and another day too in the life of their mentally deteriorating teachers.

End

The Second Cycle Marathon

1960

After last year's success the decision was made to hold a second Cycle Marathon. Red, Po and Anto were the organisers as usual. They were sitting at a table at the back of Uncle Luigi's debating the best route for the upcoming marathon. A large map of Northern Ireland covered the table and there was much discussion on which way they should go.

"I know what ya'r sayin' Anto, at least it's a shorter route than last year," said Po.
"It is for sure and just as much ta see and do as last year's route," replied Anto.
"Give me that route again," said Po.
"Ok, well the first place we come to will be Narrow Water Castle. We'll just stop there for about thirty minutes. Then it's only ten minutes to Warrenpoint. We can stay there for a couple of hours at least. From there we'll go on ta Rostrevor where we can stay for another two hours which will include a visit up ta the Cloughmore Stone and then it's

back ta the Point where we'll cut off and head ta Burren Lake. From there it's just straight home."
"That's still some cycle Anto. How far is it?" asked Red.
"It's about twenty five or so miles altogether."
"What do ya think Po?" Red asked.
"Seems ok, but we'll need to leave very early."
"Ok then, are we all agreed?" asked Red.
All heads nodded and the route was selected. They decided to leave at eight in the morning and it was Po's job to have a meeting with everyone that was going and inform them of the route and everything they should take with them.

Po informed Red and Anto the night before the Cycle Marathon that there were eleven going this year. Basically the same crowd as last year, with a few extra. Po had informed everyone what they needed to bring. It was agreed that if anyone had a puncture, everyone would stop and wait until it was mended, no one was to be left behind. All were told to make sure they had a puncture repair kit, a pump, and working lights on their bicycles.

It was Saturday morning and they were all gathered outside Uncle Luigi's on Hill Street. Everyone was there early so they were able to leave on time. The great Cycle Marathon was now under way. The group headed off towards the Warrenpoint Road, a six mile twisty road which would take them to the seaside town of Warrenpoint. They had good weather that July morning, just a few fluffy cumulus clouds slowly floating across the bright summer sky. After they had been cycling for around twenty minutes they reached Narrow Water Castle which was agreed would be their first stop.
"Who lived here Red?" asked Jumpy Jones stuffing a piece of chocolate in his mouth.
"I was readin' about this place last year. It's very old. It was originally built by a guy called Hugh de Lacy in 1212 to guard the approaches ta Newry and Uncle Luigi's Café."
"Wow, that's a long time ago."
"Yep, and over there, that's the Free State."

"Over there, ya mean them trees across the water?" said Jumpy pointing.
"Yeah, that's the South."
"Hang on a minute now," Jumpy looked around. "Then that's the west then, the way we came from, Newry?"
"No," Red pointed towards the sea. "Back towards Newry is sort of north."
Jumpy looked even more confused.
"This doesn't make sense so it doesn't. How can that be the south over there and back that way the north?"
"Jumpy, it's not the compass south, it's just the South of Ireland."
"But it's still south isn't it?"
"No, yeah, never mind, I'll get Po ta explain it ta ya. He's good at that sort of thing."
Jumpy accepted Red's compromise and wandered off to join the rest of the group who were exploring the Castle Keep and the grounds around it.
"Hi Red," shouted Po from the road.
"Yeah?"
"Ya ready ta move on?"
"Sure, next stop Warrenpoint."

Within ten minutes the group were cycling around Warrenpoint's large square where they stopped as planned to spend around an hour or two. The square was packed with pubs, cafés, ice cream parlours and of greatest interest to most of the boys, amusement arcades, which of course was the first stop.
"Hi Red, what's this?" asked Jammy.
"It's called, 'What the Butler Saw' and you're tellin' me ya don't know what it is?"
"Why the hell would a be askin'?"
"It's a murder story Jammy."
"Oh, right, thanks Red."
Red found Dunno and Kitter inspecting a machine that was full of coins on a shelf, it was called Slide Penny. When you put in a coin and you were lucky, some of the coins balancing perilously on the

shelf edge would be pushed over and the player would get them in the payout slot.
"What in the name a God are you two up ta?" asked Red.
"Settin' up this machine."
"What de ya mean, settin' it up?"
"Wait a minute, Jumpy's goin' ta cause a diversion."
Suddenly there was a crash and Jumpy could be seen sprawled on the floor where he had apparently fallen. The staff all rushed to Jumpy's aid. Kitter and Dunno quickly moved behind the machine and with some effort managed to tilt it slightly forward. There was a loud clatter of money dropping into the payout slot. The coins arriving were removed with considerable speed, pocketed and the two players moved off without a word to explore some more machines. Red caught up with Po who was playing a fruit machine with Anto.
"Did ya see them friggers?" he asked.
"Stupid Jumpy fallin'?" Anto asked.
Red related the story to them. They both laughed.
"I'm just delighted so I am. These things are rigged so they are," complained Po.
"Where are we for next?" asked Anto.
"Well, I think it's ta get some food from the café and then to the park for a bit."
"Sounds good, are we ready ta go?"
"Yeah, give them ejits a call will ya?"

After getting the burgers and chips etc., they ended up in the Warrenpoint Municipal Park, an area of well kept lawns and many varieties of colourful flowers. Since no Park Keeper could be seen it was decided to play a game of football. This lasted almost twenty minutes until the keeper turned up and chased them from the park. The friendly game resulted in four bruised shins, a lump on the head, two sprained ankles, and a suspected broken toe.

They moved off again on their way to the beautiful village of Rostrevor, which rests peacefully at the foot of the towering dark Mourne Mountains. The cycle to Rostrevor followed the coast road within sight of the sea all the way. The sun glistened on the calm Carlingford Lough

making the whole scene almost surreal. The first stop after negotiating the quaint narrow streets of Rostrevor, was a beautiful stream trickling over ancient stones and continuing its journey under a lovely humpback granite bridge on its way to the sea. This was called the Fairy Glen. They stayed there for about thirty minutes. Red, Anto and Po were seated on a bench eating apples and watching the boys, now barefooted, messing about on the stones that caused cascades in the stream.
"Ya know what's gonna happen, don't ya?" said Anto to Red.
There was a loud yell, closely followed by a great splash.
"Yeah, and it just did," laughed Red.
Shifty McShane was sitting in the stream; hands outspread looking down at himself while all his pals greatly comforted him with sympathetic laughter.

Next the group headed off on the climb through the beautiful Rostrevor forest up the steep mountain track to reach the famous Cloughmore Stone. For most of the route the boys had to walk with their bikes, however, eventually they made it to the summit. The views from here could only be described as breathtaking. The panoramic view of Carlingford Lough, afforded them an almost perfect picture of the coastline as far as Warrenpoint. On the other side they could see from Omeath, right along the coast to Carlingford and all the way to Greenore. The lough was guarded on both sides by great mountain ranges. On the north side stood the majestic dark Mournes and on the south side the rocky Cooley's. The boys enjoyed the great view for almost an hour. When everyone had managed to get a small rock landed on top of the Cloughmore Stone, as was the tradition, they proceeded back down the mountain to Rostrevor.

Heading back the way they came they returned to Warrenpoint and turned right on the road to Burren. In a short time they reached the Burren Lake where they stopped and spent a pleasant hour or so lying on the fishermen's walkways trying to spot trout or eels. Finally it was time to head for home. The sun was low in the sky and the temperature had dropped quite considerably. They headed back in the direction of Warrenpoint turning right onto the lovely, twisting, tree covered Mound Road which took them back to Narrow Water Castle. It was decided to make an unscheduled stop and visit the forest that runs from the Warrenpoint Road back up the hillside. Finding a nice place to stop, they were all in the forest in minutes clambering up trees, playing Cowboys and Indians, pretending to be Tarzan and so on. Finally, after another hour of frivolity, cuts, sprains, grazed knees and elbows, the energy levels had taken a final dip. So at 9.30pm the tired cyclists arrived back in Newry. Goodbyes were mumbled, and all went on their weary way home. Red and Po decided to stop for five minutes in Uncle Luigi's with Anto for a coffee.

"Well, did ya enjoy today?" Anto asked Po.
"De ya know, there's not a single one of that crowd that's the full shillin'," answered Po.
"Are ya only seein' that now?" laughed Red.
"Most of them should be locked up ya know?" Po went on.
"Ah sure they're only childer ya know," smiled Anto.
"Hairy arsed childer," laughed Po. "De ya know what we should do? Next year we should bring camping gear and take a proper cycle marathon, ya know, stay away for a weekend."
"Are ya outta your wee head. We'd need ta bring a doctor and nurse with us," said Red.
"De ya know any that would go?" asked Po seriously.
Poor Po got punched from both sides.

End

The Street Wars

1960

It was a warm spring afternoon on the Armagh Road in Newry. Red, Anto and Jammy were walking down the gentle hill toward the centre of Newry on their way home from school.

"Red, Anto, wait up," came the voice of Po, who was running to catch up with them. When he did so, he was breathing heavily and took a minute to release his news to his mates.

"They, want, a war, tomorrow," he managed to get out.

"Who does?" asked Anto.

"High Street."

"How do ya know?" asked Red.

"Got the word from wee Gerry Hughes, just now."

"Where?" asked Jammy.

"Up the rocks, at three o'clock."

"Jasus, that's not a lot of notice. We have to get everybody together and come up with a plan of attack by tomorrow? They're friggin' up ta somethin'," mused Anto.

"The question is, are we goin' ta accept? If we say no, we'll never hear the end of it," added Red.

"Ta hell with them, let's take the bastards," snarled Jammy.

"Well, I'm up for it. We need ta call an emergency meeting of the War Council," said Anto.
"Get the word out ta everyone. We'll meet at Uncle Luigi's, at seven tonight, ok?" suggested Red.
All agreed.

Seven of the War Council turned up for the meeting. The only one missing was Shifty, who had diarrhoea. Anto was the Chairman, and called the meeting to order.
"Right. Now High Street wants a war with us at the Rocks tomorrow, at three. I need ta know if we are goin', ta meet them, and if so, can we get a plan of action together quick enough? Those who are for takin' them on, raise your hands."
The vote was unanimous, in favour of war.
"At this time I will call on Po, the Weapons and Strategy Officer, to say a few words."

Po stood up and went to the head of the gathering. He looked very officious.
"Now, as for weapons I will need those of ya who supplied the ammo last time to do it again. Jumpy, will ya get the rotten fruit from Boyle's in the mornin'? Shifty usually got the rotten eggs, so who will get those?"
"Ya can leave that with me," said Blackie. "I have ta go ta Murphy's in the mornin', anyway."
"Anto, will ya get plenty of slops from the kitchen?" asked Po.
"The bins are full at the moment," smiled Anto.
"Ok, I will work on a plan of action tonight and have it ready by lunchtime, tomorrow," added Po.
"Bishop, don't ya know that wee guy Sheridan, from High Street?" asked Anto.
"Yeah, he's a good mate."
"Well now, let's see how good a mate he is. Get hold of him today and see if he can find out what the High Street crowd are plannin'."
"Will do."
"Ok, so that's it for now," said Anto.

"Right. Now lads, we will meet here tomorrow at lunchtime, ok?" said Anto, standing up.
There were nods and grunts of agreement.

The rules of Street Wars were very strict. There were seven gangs who took part in these wars: Castle Street, High Street, Dromalane, Boat Street, China Town, O'Neill Avenue and Church Street. Two gangs, at a pre-arranged time and place, would line up about 100 yards apart. In the middle there was a clearly-marked dividing line, or 'border'. Each gang had their own flag, which would be planted in the ground, 50 yards on their side of the border. The idea was for the opposing gang, or enemy, to capture the flag. When this was done, the war was over. Each side was allowed to use what was known as 'soft ammo'. This could be rotten tomatoes, eggs, fruit, slops of any kind, water, mud, etc. to beat the other side back, far enough to capture their flag. There were some ingenious ideas tried over the years, like pits filled with slops and covered with thin branches and sods to trap the enemy. Po had been working on a number of ideas which he had not yet tried out, so it looked like tomorrow he would get a chance to use one, and hope it worked.

After the meeting Red, Po, Anto and Jammy were sitting in the first snug.
"What ideas have ya Po?" Red asked.
"I have been workin' on a real stormer," smiled Po.
"What is it?" asked Anto.
"I call it the 'The Glar Offence'."
"So, what the frig is it, then?" asked Red.
"I'm not goin' in ta details just now, till I get it totally worked out in ma mind, ok?"
"The deep thinker, huh?"
"I need about five or six of the lads to get as many containers as they can and meet me at the park on the Warrenpoint Road, about six o'clock."

That evening, Po met up with six of the gang on the Warrenpoint Road, as planned. Each one had brought along, as ordered, receptacles, like large cans, tin baths, buckets etc.
"Ok Po, we're all here now. What are we gonna put in these buckets?"
"Glar."
"Glar?"
"Glar."
"Jasus, that stuff stinks.....Po, sure ya'r a wee genius," laughed Red.

Glar was the local name for a black mud left behind by the tide. It was covered in a skin of shining silver and was usually at least twelve inches deep. It had a smell similar to rotten eggs mixed with excreta and many other similar aromas. The gang approached the edge of the river Clanrye, which led into the Carlingford Lough and the Irish Sea. At this time the tide was out and the glar was easily accessible. When all the containers were full the gang headed back toward the town.

"I take it we will be usin' this as ammo, then?" said Anto to Po.
"That's the idea, but it's how we use it will be the winning of the war," smiled Po.
"Well tell us, then," snarled Red, who was struggling with a large tin of glar.
"I left the stuff a need in your back yard this mornin'. When we get there I'll show ya how I hope this will work."

Ten minutes later the gang was in Red's back yard and sitting down after their long walk from the Warrenpoint Road and the river.
"Now, this is a tube from a tractor wheel," said Po, holding up a long piece of rubber,
"We are goin' ta get two stakes in the ground and make the world's biggest catapult."
"Jasus, isn't that somethin'," commented Jumpy.
"What are ya plannin' to use for stakes?" asked Red.
"Ah, these," said Po, as he lifted a long, pointed, thick fence post.
"We will use a sledge hammer to get them well into the ground, fix the tractor tubes to the two stakes and we are ready to go. As ya can see I

have used our fella's glue ta put some extra rubber on the middle, so it will hold more."
Every member of the gang had a smile on his face, thinking of their great new weapon in action against the enemy.
"Po, what's the paint and sheet for?" asked Anto.
"Well, this is where we have to be clever, ya see. We are just goin' ta paint Castle Street on the sheet like it was a banner, but ya see, we'll be holdin' it in front of our catapult, so the enemy won't see it," smiled Po.
"Po, sure aren't ya the devious wee bastard, altogether," grinned Red.
"And proud of it. Come on; let's get this stuff together now."

****

The gang, now numbering fifteen, were already on the High Street Rocks, getting themselves ready for the coming battle. They were all dressed in their ragged jeans and trousers, torn shirts, and shoes falling apart. No one was going to wear good clothing for a war! The Rocks, 400 yards long and with a 500 foot steep grass-covered slope to the top, was located behind the houses on High Street. From the top, a beautiful panoramic view of the town of Newry was available. Because the summit was plateau-like, it was used for football and many other games.

Bishop had contacted his friend from High Street who told him that as far as he was aware, the High Street gang had no set plan for the war, other than the usual attack with soft ammo. He did say, however, that he thought that their numbers had increased quite a lot, possibly, well over twenty. They were just planning a frontal attack and believed their numbers would win the day.

Quite a large audience gathered for these wars, which were looked upon by the locals as great entertainment. Supporters from both sides, moms, dads, uncles, brothers, sisters, girlfriends, potential girlfriends, would gather on the sidelines and cheer their heroes on. It was now five minutes to three. The leaders of both armies walked to the border and shook hands. The Castle Street leader was Anto and the High

Street leader being Billy 'The Liar' Gallagher. The terms of the war were agreed, as usual, and at exactly three, the war would begin. Each side planted their flags in the ground and waited. The great sheet banner was rippling in the breeze, but doing its job of hiding the now ready-to-use catapult.

The watches on both sides informed their owners that it was three o'clock. The yells of 'Charge' came from both sides. When the sides got within 30 feet of each other they began using their ammo carried in buckets, tins, old school bags, etc. The Castle Street army did not throw as much as they normally would, under the instructions of Anto. In a very short time they had, indeed, begun to retreat, to the delight of the High Street contingent, who surged forward, still throwing ammo at their retreating foe.

When the High Street army was within twenty feet of the Castle Street banner the voice of Anto could be heard yelling, 'down, down'. The retreating army dropped to the ground at the same time the banner was lifted away. The High Street Army slowed somewhat, not knowing what was going on. When they looked up they saw the great catapult pulled back by Red, Po, and two others, with smiles on their faces. Suddenly, a great blob of black stuff hit the front row of the High Street Army with some force, knocking them to the ground, leaving them totally covered, from head to toe, in the black, sticky, smelly glar. A second round of the same was on its way and hit the stunned second row, knocking them to the ground, also. The rest of the High Street Army seeing what had happened to their mates decided they wanted none of it, and took to their heels as fast as they could go, in the opposite direction. Anto's voice could be heard above the shouts of the enemy, 'charge'. Now the Castle Street Army was throwing everything they had at the enemy, who was running away in some disorder. The High Street flag was snatched by the Bishop, and held in the air to the cheering of the Castle Street Army.
The Castle Street Army gathered after they had seen off the last of the enemy.

"Right, everybody, back to the café. I think this occasion calls for free chips for everyone," smiled Anto. A loud cheer followed.
"Hold on a minute Anto. As inventor of the glar catapult, I should be getting fish, as well."
Anto rubbed his chin and looked at Red.
"He has a point, ya know, Red. We should give him something special for his part in today's great victory, shouldn't we?"
"Ya'r absolutely right, Anto, Po really deserves something special. Would ya by any chance be thinkin' along the same lines as my own self?"
"I do believe there is a meetin' of the minds here."
Red and Anto, both moving together, grabbed Po. Anto got his kicking feet and Red, his twisting squealing upper body. Po was unceremoniously lowered into a large bath of leftover glar. Red and Anto later discussed the incident and both agreed that Po's vocabulary of expletives was indeed quite impressive.

End

The Legend of the Four Nuns

1960

The boys had been playing football that July night and on returning from the little park on the Warrenpoint Road decided to go to the fields behind the St. John of God's Hospital which were known as 'The Back Fields'. After messing around for over an hour it was beginning to get quite dark.
They all ended up sitting under a semi fallen tree which was leaning on another.
"Red, tell us a ghost story," said Jammy. A chorus of approval came from all the others.
Red enjoyed telling ghost stories of which he knew many. Paying close attention was Po, Jammy, Dunno, Kitter, the Bishop and Ginger.

"Well ok then, I'll tell yous the one about the Four Nuns," said Red making himself comfortable.
"This, by the way, is a true story. It came from the old storyteller Charlie O'Donaghue himself and told ta me by ma grandda. Hundreds of years ago, when the British were here, in Newry, they had some kind

of dislike for the Nuns ya see. Anyway, as the story goes, it was a very stormy night when they broke into the Nun's home and dragged four of them out into this very field. They were charged, it was said, with helpin' those who were against the British in Ireland. It was a dark and creepy sort of night," said Red slowly looking around.
"They strung up the Nuns to that tree," said Red pointing to the fallen tree, "and hanged them."
Red waited, using the dramatic pause well. He looked up at the tree, now lowering his voice to a whisper.
"It has been said if ya look close on a night like tonight, ya can actually see the shadows of the Nuns, swayin' from the branches, ya can hear the ropes creakin'." He stopped again and looked at the circle of faces in the dim light now staring up at the leaning tree. Red clapped his hands, everyone jumped, startled.
"Lightnin' struck the tree while the soldiers were standin' there laughin' at the dyin' Nuns. They laughed no more, for it killed every last one of them. The tree, as ya can see, toppled and came ta rest against that one there," Red stopped again for a dramatic pause. "Many, many times the Nuns have been seen here in this field wanderin' about, sort of a glow comin' from them it is said. Sometimes people have sat here where we are right now, looked up and saw…" Red hesitated, lowered his voice and continued… "blood runnin' down the tree," he said, very slowly for effect.
"Sometimes on a night like tonight the Nuns would suddenly appear when the wind got up," he looked around slowly. Almost as if on cue a strong gust of wind rustled the bushes and trees around them. Red heard some noise and lifted his head to discover he was on his own. His audience had taken off at great speed without a parting word. Not panicking or anything like that, he rose quickly, and took off at a pace that surprised even himself. He was able to catch up with the boys who had a good hundred yards head start as they reached Courtney Hill.

When they got back to the lights of Castle Street, they stopped and sat on the steps at the top of Hyde Market, all panting and sucking air in great gulps. "Why the hell did you shits take off?" panted Red. "Are ya serious," said Po. "I had visions of them Nuns hanging from that tree and lookin' at me."

"He's right ya know, I'm nearly sure a heard a rope creakin' so I am," said Jammy.
"Well, whatever, I'm glad we got ta hell outta that place," added Po. "It was friggin' creepy."
"It was just when ya were talkin' about the blood runnin down the tree and this big gust a wind started. Jasus it scared the shit outta me," said Jammy.
"I'm glad we got outta there my own self," finished Red. "Not the sorta place ya want ta be hangin' around."

There were glances exchanged and almost on cue they all broke into well welcomed laughter.

End

Colour Blind

1960

As Red was walking into Uncle Luigi's he heard his name being called. Turning, he saw Roberto behind the Ice Cream counter beckoning him.
"Hi Roberto, what's happenin'?"
"Red will ya do me a favour?"
"Sure, what?"
"I got a stupid scratch on the car and I need some spray paint to cover it. Will ya go around to Brown's and get some for me?"
"No problem. What do I ask for?"
"Tell them ya want black spray paint and tell them it's for a Ford. Make sure ya say that ok? Here's the money."
"Ok, I'll remember, be back soon."

Red left the Café and walked to Brown's Auto Supplies on Water Street. As he entered he noticed John Mullan behind the counter.
"Hi John."
"Red, how's yourself, haven't seen ya in ages."
"Not too bad, sure I'm just strugglin' bravely."
"Ach sure God help ya. What are ya lookin' for?"

"Well, it's for Roberto Falsoni. He got a scratch on the car and wants a can of spray paint. It's black and he told me ta make sure I told ya, it's for a Ford."
"Let's have a look then." John came around the counter and went to a display stand in the middle of the shop. After a few moments he found the paint, returned behind the counter, put the paint in a bag and handed it to Red.
"There ya go, half crown."
Red handed over the money, thanked John and left.

Ten minutes later he walked into Uncle Luigi's. Looking around he could not see Roberto.
He walked to the top counter, where Anto was serving.
"Where's Roberto?"
"He's just gone to pick up some spuds. He'll be back in ten minutes."
"I was just gettin' some paint for him."
"For the car? Yeah, he told me he sent ya. Did ya get it ok?"
"Yeah."
Red sat down in one of the snugs after ordering a coffee. He opened the bag and took out the can of paint to look at it. After a short inspection he gasped as he read the label.
"Oh shit, what a stupid bastard."
Anto was arriving as Red put the paint back into the bag.
"That stupid bastard John Mullan has just gone and gave me the wrong friggin' paint. Now a have ta go all the way back, frig it."
"Such is life. Poor Red, sure God help ya," smiled Anto.
"Yeah, right," mumbled Red taking a sip of his coffee and getting up.

****

"Jasus, back again? I don't see ya for a year, then twice in the same day," smiled John. "Hey Matt, is there a special discount for Red buying twice in the same day?"
"Charge the bugger double," smiled Matt, the owner as he approached.
"Hello Red, playin' any football these days?"

"Hi Matt, yeah, I'm still with West End but hope ta be movin' next season."
"Ya could do better for sure. What ya lookin' for?"
"See that auld ejit there," smiled Red pointing at John.
"I came in earlier looking for black spray paint for a Ford. He only goes and gives me brown."
"Show me."
Red handed the bag to Matt, who removed the paint from the bag and inspected it.
"John come over here ta ya see this."
Matt showed the paint tin to John who also inspected it. They both burst out laughing.
"Red," said Matt putting his arm around Red's shoulder.
"Come on with me outside ta a show ya somethin'."
When they got outside Matt turned Red around facing the shop front.
"How long have ya lived in Newry?"
"Jasus, all my life, 15 years, why?"
"An, how many times have ya been in my shop?"
"Dozens, why?"
"Look up there Red. See that big writin' above the door. Would ya read it for me?"
Red looked puzzled. He looked up at the shop name and began to read.
"Matt Brown, ah no, Jasus, no. I couldn't have, no."
"Ya see Red, Matt Brown is the name of the shop, not the paint. That is our wee label on the can ya see."
Red could feel his face reddening as he stood looking up at the sign. John had now joined them outside.
"Well Red, de ya want a tin of Matt Brown too?" he roared.
"Ah Jasus, I cannot believe I did this. John, Matt, if ya tell any of the lads about this I'll be ruined. I'll haunt yis."
"Ya auld ejit, are ya crackin' up or what?" laughed Matt.
"He must be in love Matt," laughed John leaning against the shop front to steady himself.
"Jasus, I can't believe I did this, I just can't believe it," mumbled Red covering his face with both hands. This of course did not in any way

help Matt and John, if anything it made them worse. Matt was holding his side, John was leaning against the window. Red looked at them. His embarrassment had only deepened. He had to get away.
"I'm just off. I'm goin' ta throw myself in the canal, are yis happy now?" snapped Red. This was just too much for his two roaring friends. Both were now sitting on the footpath.
Red walked back to Uncle Luigi's looking at the ground. He kept mumbling to himself all the way. When he arrived Roberto was back behind the counter.

"Did ya get it ok?"
"Yeah, I got it, no problem," Red mumbled.
He sat down in one of the snugs just as Po arrived.
"Well, I was in lookin' for ya earlier. Anto said ya were off gettin' paint for Roberto."
"Yeah, I was."
"So?"
"So what?"
"Did ya get it ok?"
"I got it, I got it. Why are ya so interested?"
"Knowin' you ya wally, ya probably got brown instead of black," laughed Po.
Red just stared at Po and smiled.
"Ya know Po. Ya might well know me a lot better than ya think ya do."

End